The thought of losing her scared him.

Damn it, where was she? He had to find her. When he did, there would be no more lies between them. He'd tell her the truth about everything—about Legate, the surveillance and Jeremy's death.

Amid the pedestrians on the opposite side of the street, he caught a glimpse of white-blond hair. Anya! He dashed across the street toward her.

Though she appeared to be alone, Roman couldn't be sure. The CIA might have her under surveillance. And there was always the danger that Legate security was watching.

He should have been more subtle in his approach, but he couldn't hold back. His instinct was to protect her, to gather her up and take her somewhere safe. He touched her arm, reassuring himself that she was real.

When she gazed at him, her blue eyes were watery and confused. "Roman? What are you doing here?"

Dear Harlequin Intrigue Reader,

Temperatures are rising this month at Harlequin Intrigue! So whether our mesmerizing men of action are steaming up their love lives or packing heat in high-stakes situations, July's lineup is guaranteed to sizzle!

Back by popular demand is the newest branch of our Confidential series. Meet the heroes of NEW ORLEANS CONFIDENTIAL—tough undercover operatives who will stop at nothing to rid the streets of a crime ring tied to the most dangerous movers and shakers in town. *USA TODAY* bestselling author Rebecca York launches the series with *Undercover Encounter*—a darkly sensual tale about a secret agent who uses every resource at his disposal to get his former flame out alive when she goes deep undercover in the sultry French Quarter.

The highly acclaimed Gayle Wilson returns to the lineup with *Sight Unseen*. In book three of PHOENIX BROTHERHOOD, it's a race against time to prevent a powerful terrorist organization from unleashing unspeakable harm. Prepare to become entangled in *Velvet Ropes* by Patricia Rosemoor—book three in CLUB UNDERCOVER— when a clandestine investigation plunges a couple into danger....

Our sassy inline continuity SHOTGUN SALLYS ends with a bang! You won't want to miss *Lawful Engagement* by Linda O. Johnston. In Cassie Miles's newest Harlequin Intrigue title—*Protecting the Innocent*—a widow trapped in a labyrinth of evil brings out the Achilles' heel in a duplicitous man of mystery.

Delores Fossen's newest thriller is not to be missed. *Veiled Intentions* arouses searing desires when two bickering cops pose as doting fiancés in their pursuit of a deranged sniper!

Enjoy our explosive lineup this month!

Denise O'Sullivan
Senior Editor, Harlequin Intrigue

PROTECTING THE INNOCENT

CASSIE MILES

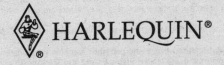

HARLEQUIN®

TORONTO • NEW YORK • LONDON
AMSTERDAM • PARIS • SYDNEY • HAMBURG
STOCKHOLM • ATHENS • TOKYO • MILAN • MADRID
PRAGUE • WARSAW • BUDAPEST • AUCKLAND

ISBN 0-373-22787-6

PROTECTING THE INNOCENT

This edition published by arrangement with Harlequin Books S.A.

® and TM are trademarks of the publisher. Trademarks indicated with ® are registered in the United States Patent and Trademark Office, the Canadian Trade Marks Office and in other countries.

www.eHarlequin.com

Printed in U.S.A.

ABOUT THE AUTHOR

Exercise is not a favorite occupation for Denver resident Cassie Miles, but she does try to walk every morning. On one snowy morning, she was "exercising" with a friend in Cherry Creek Mall. They paused to fill out a contest entry form at Neiman Marcus, and her friend *won* a first-class trip for an afternoon tea at any Neiman Marcus store. They chose San Francisco. This trip provided much of the research for *Protecting the Innocent*, though neither of these ladies found true love. Room service at the Ritz-Carlton was a great consolation prize.

Books by Cassie Miles

HARLEQUIN INTRIGUE
122—HIDE AND SEEK
150—HANDLE WITH CARE
237—HEARTBREAK HOTEL
269—ARE YOU LONESOME
      TONIGHT?
285—DON'T BE CRUEL
320—MYSTERIOUS VOWS
332—THE SUSPECT GROOM
363—THE IMPOSTER
381—RULE BREAKER
391—GUARDED MOMENTS
402—A NEW YEAR'S
      CONVICTION
443—A REAL ANGEL
449—FORGET ME NOT
521—FATHER, LOVER, BODYGUARD
529—THE SAFE HOSTAGE
584—UNDERCOVER PROTECTOR
645—STATE OF EMERGENCY†
649—WEDDING CAPTIVES†
670—NOT ON HIS WATCH
694—THE SECRET SHE KEEPS
769—RESTLESS SPIRIT
787—PROTECTING THE INNOCENT

HARLEQUIN
AMERICAN ROMANCE
567—BUFFALO McCLOUD
574—BORROWED TIME

HARLEQUIN TEMPTATION
 61—ACTS OF MAGIC
104—IT'S ONLY NATURAL
170—SEEMS LIKE OLD TIMES
235—MONKEY BUSINESS
305—UNDER LOCK AND KEY
394—A RISKY PROPOSITION

†Colorado Search and Rescue

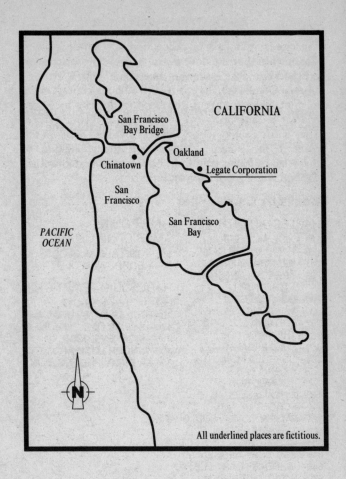

CALIFORNIA

San Francisco
Bay Bridge

Oakland

Chinatown

Legate Corporation

San
Francisco

PACIFIC
OCEAN

San Francisco
Bay

N

All underlined places are fictitious.

CAST OF CHARACTERS

Roman Alexander—The dashing head administrator at the Legate Corporation think tank leads a dangerous double life.

Anya Bouchard Parrish—After her husband's death, she seeks the simple pleasures of life. Instead, she finds intrigue and danger.

Charlie Parrish—Anya's five-year-old son is gifted with genius-level intelligence.

Jeremy Parrish—Anya's scientist husband died in a suspicious accident. Was it murder?

Fredrick Slater—The head of the Legate Corporation seeks the "greater good" and ignores the consequences.

Dr. Lowell Neville—The company psychiatrist engages in questionable research procedures.

Wade Bouchard—Anya's idealistic father abandoned the family when she was a child.

Claudette Bouchard—Anya's brilliant mother is retired from a demanding career as an international consultant.

Jane Coopersmith—The Legate receptionist knows everything about everybody.

To Lesly Pogrew Terrance, a winner.
And, as always, for Rick.

Prologue

Roman Alexander ran alone on the packed sand of the narrow beach. A patina of morning dew coated the surface of his thermal black running suit and dampened his thick black hair. He picked up the pace, churning through the heavy fog off San Francisco Bay, running harder. Exercise without exertion was useless. To build his strength and stamina, he challenged his physical limits.

Changing stride, he ascended the eighty-seven winding stairs up the cliffside to the grounds of the Legate Corporation. At the top, he hit the asphalt footpath, which was exactly five point eight miles in length.

Across the rolling lawn, he could see the outline of the main headquarters, a sprawling gray stone mansion built more than a hundred and twenty years ago on this prime bay-front real estate south of Oakland. When he first came to work here as chief administrator and vice president, he thought of the mansion as a castle. Legate was his realm— one of the foremost think tanks in the nation. Their motto was For The Greater Good. And Roman had believed it. Years ago. Now, those gray stone walls seemed as ominous as the guard towers of a prison.

At Building Fourteen near the front entrance to the gated grounds, he took a detour, slowed his pace to a jog and entered. This squat, ugly structure—little more than a barracks—had always been intended as a temporary headquarters, and tomorrow the physicists and biochemists who worked here would complete their transfer to a large, state-of-the-art permanent facility nearer the mansion.

The sterile white hallway bisecting Building Fourteen was cluttered with packing crates. Many had already made the move.

Roman shoved open the door to an office beside the biochemistry lab. As he expected, Jeremy Parrish was still here, hard at work. He was a good man, a trusted friend. Sitting behind his desk, he scribbled furiously in a spiral notebook.

"Use the laptop," Roman said.

"Gotta see it on paper first." Without looking up, Jeremy kept writing.

"Should I instruct the movers to crate you up and carry you across the grounds?" Roman asked.

With a flourish, Jeremy completed his notation. He seemed ill. His complexion had taken on a sickly pale sheen, like the underbelly of a trout.

"You're working too hard," Roman said. "You look like hell."

"No big deal. There's some kind of flu floating around the lab."

It was an incredibly vague comment from a respected scientist with a doctorate in biochemistry, a man who regularly dealt with complex viral and bacterial infections.

"Besides," Jeremy said, "I want to complete this project fast so I can get back to Denver."

His gaze slid across the cluttered desk to a photograph of his wife, Anya, and their four-year-old son. Roman picked up the framed picture of a healthy toddler and a bashfully smiling woman with long, straight, white-blond hair. He'd always admired Anya. Though she appeared delicate and ephemeral, her blue eyes snapped with intelligence and humor. She was always ready to laugh, always up for a challenge. If she hadn't married his friend, Roman might have gone after her for himself, giving up his reputation as one of the most eligible bachelors in the Bay Area. "You're a lucky man, Jeremy."

"Don't I know it. I never thought I'd be able to have children. And little Charlie——" He broke off, coughing. "That kid is the light of my life."

Little Charlie was the primary reason Jeremy had agreed to work at Legate on specialized projects. It was Legate's discoveries and experimentations that had paved the way for Anya's successful in vitro fertilization.

When Jeremy coughed again, Roman said, "That sounds bad. You should take some time off."

"I can't believe what I'm hearing." Jeremy forced a grin. "Is it possible? Is Roman Alexander, the administrative slave driver, suggesting that one of his scientists take time off?"

Roman grinned back at him. Very few people would dare to smart mouth to him. But his relationship with Jeremy was different. They'd known each other since they were both on the high school track team. Roman achieved a statewide record in the 500 meters that remained unbroken. Jeremy had been a pole vaulter.

"Somebody has to look after you eggheads," Roman said. "If I didn't come over here and rattle your test tubes occasionally, you'd forget to eat."

"I'll have this project done by the end of the week. Then I'll have a month, maybe two, in Denver with Anya and Charlie."

"Or you could book a flight out today," Roman suggested. "This formula of yours isn't exactly a world-shattering priority."

"I beg to differ. This antiseptic cleansing agent will prevent infection, especially in makeshift Third World clinics where—"

"It's soap, Jeremy."

"Maybe you're right. I should go home and get well." He sat behind his desk. "Right after I finish this last computation. Shouldn't take more than an hour or so."

If Roman had a woman like Anya waiting for him, he'd have flown out the door. He waved goodbye to his dedicated friend. "Say hi to Anya and Charlie for me."

"You bet."

Roman left the office and dodged around the clutter in the hallway. After this move was complete, he might take a little time off himself. He needed a break, and the sexy lady lawyer he'd been dating had dropped a couple hints about how much she'd enjoy a long weekend of skiing in Squaw Valley.

Outside, the fog had lifted only slightly. The promise of another dank, dreary day made the sunlit ski slopes with glistening white snow seem even more appealing.

Halfway up the incline toward the mansion, the ground rumbled beneath his custom-made running shoes. An earthquake? Then he heard the explosions.

Building Fourteen shattered in three bursts of red flame. Bits of glass shimmered in the sudden intense heat. Chunks of concrete from the foundation soared then crashed to earth. The wooden frame of the building splintered into matchsticks.

Acting on instinct, Roman charged back toward the lab, toward the door he'd left only moments ago. But there was no door. No building. Only a raging wall of flame. He darted close, but the heat drove him back, stinging his eyes. Harsh black smoke seared his lungs.

He had to get inside the fire. It was his job to take care of these scientists. He wouldn't let them die. He ducked down and crawled closer.

Crimson embers burned holes in his running suit. Nothing could survive this heat, but he had to try, had to impose his iron will on the force of the explosion.

Someone pulled him back. Dizzy from inhaling the acrid smoke, Roman didn't have the strength to resist. He sat back on his heels and stared.

Jeremy! God, no! This can't be.

Chapter One

"This is what Jeremy wanted." Claudette Bouchard spoke in her usual authoritative tone.

"I know, Mother." Anya Bouchard Parrish stared down at her hands, folded calmly in her lap as if her heart weren't racing.

"These were your husband's instructions."

Her mother paced in the executive office at the Legate mansion on her birdlike legs. Claudette was a petite, tidy woman—utterly organized, from her color-coordinated pumps to her French twist hairdo.

Next to her mother, Anya always felt like a clumsy giantess though she was only five feet eight inches tall. She pushed a messy wing of blond hair away from her cheek.

Claudette snapped, "Why are you hesitating?"

Because Anya still couldn't believe that her loving, sensitive husband had made these provisions in his will without mentioning his plans to her. *Why? Why hadn't they discussed this?*

Her gaze lifted, and she stared across the marble desktop toward Fredrick Slater, the founder and CEO of the Legate Corporation. Beneath his steel-gray mane, Slater's craggy features softened as he regarded her with sympathy—an expression that had become all too familiar. Anya was a thirty-two-year-old widow with a five-year-old son. Everyone felt sorry for her; none could assuage her grief.

"Ánya," her mother said impatiently. "We're all trying to do the right thing. For Charlie's sake."

The right thing? A bitter sigh died in her throat. Nothing had been "right" since Jeremy was killed eight months ago in Building Fourteen on these very grounds. She might have blamed Slater for the tragedy that claimed the lives of four scientists and two maintenance people, but the explosion was investigated and deemed an accident. While Building Fourteen was in the process of being closed down, the gas main was supposed to be disconnected. But there was a leak. And then...

Without wanting to, she imagined the burst of flame, the shattering force of utter annihilation—a vision that haunted her nightmares. Roman's description had been too vivid, but she'd asked him to tell her about it. She needed to know the details, to somehow understand this horrifying, incomprehensible disaster.

The stillborn sigh escaped her lips. Sometimes, her loss weighed like an anchor, dragging her down. Anya didn't know how she would have made it this far without Roman's unflagging support.

Eight months ago, he accompanied the casket with Jeremy's charred remains back to Denver for the funeral. Though she knew Roman was a busy executive, he took time off from Legate and stayed in Denver for weeks, entertaining Charlie and offering his shoulder for her to cry upon. She'd drawn from his strength.

More than anyone else, he shared her sorrow. After he returned to Legate, his e-mails and phone calls were always a comfort, seeming to come at those moments when she missed Jeremy the most.

She thought it odd that Roman hadn't contacted her

when she and Charlie arrived last night. Their plane was met at the Oakland Airport by a Legate limo.

She looked toward Slater and asked, "Where's Roman?"

"Out of town," he said. "We had an emergency in L.A. that required his immediate attention."

"Will he be back today?"

"Most likely." Leaning forward on his desktop, Slater laced his fingers together. Though he wasn't a big man, his hands were large with fingers so long, he was probably capable of playing Rachmaninoff. "Do you have specific questions, Anya?"

"A few." She rose from the leather chair facing his desk and went to the arched, second-story window overlooking the Legate grounds. The October grass had faded, and the live oak and elm had begun to turn. Though she couldn't see the waters of the bay beyond the forested landscaping, moisture hung in the air, creating an idyllic mist.

Directly below the window was a hedge maze, and she spotted Charlie. Her small son dragged the woman who had been assigned to keep an eye on him through the twisting pathways toward a marble fountain in the center. Charlie paused for only a second at each turn, calculating the probabilities that led to the correct route. He made few mistakes and never once retraced an error.

A fond smile touched Anya's lips, and her heart swelled with pride. Her son was exceptionally bright with an IQ at the genius level. Not that his high intelligence was a surprise. Jeremy had been brilliant. Anya's mother had an M.D. and Ph.D., and her father was a physicist—as brilliant as he was irresponsible, having abandoned her and her mother before Anya's third birthday.

Claudette fluttered up behind her. "Stop wasting time. You need to sign these documents."

Stubbornly, Anya continued to stare through the window. This was an important decision, and she wouldn't be rushed. "Please don't think I'm ungrateful, Mr. Slater. Your offer is generous and, I'm sure, well-intentioned."

"Not completely unselfish," he admitted. "If Charlie is educated here, under the tutelage of Legate instructors, I believe your son will evolve into one of the finest minds of this century."

"But will he have the chance to be a kid?"

Her mother scoffed. Claudette never put much stock in the everyday pleasures of childhood. "That's such nonsense."

"But important to me." Anya turned away from the window to face her mother. "Kids need to be able to spend an afternoon lying in the grass and staring up at the clouds. Getting dirty. Playing baseball. Maybe even being a pole vaulter like his dad."

"We have facilities for extracurricular activity," Slater said. "You've already seen the stables and the swimming pool."

"Right."

"And if you want Charlie to spend time cloud-gazing, that's fine. You're in charge of his free time. You're still his mother."

"What about playtime with other children?" Anya asked.

"As you know," Slater said, "we have five other children in the program."

Anya knew that the five other kids ranged in age from four to seven. All had been carefully screened before being accepted into the Legate program. All had IQs at the genius level.

"I can't imagine why you're hesitating," her mother said. "If you stayed in Denver, you'd likely have to go back to work, and Charlie would be wasting his time in a day-care center. Think of your son, Anya. My grandson. He deserves the chance to develop his full potential.''

But this arrangement seemed unnatural. Even though Anya would retain her guardianship of Charlie, Legate would take care of everything else. They'd educate him and provide a home for both of them. Anya would even be paid a stipend. For what? For being his mother? She hated that idea.

''What about *my* life?'' she said. ''What if I decide to get married again?''

''Didn't you read the contract?'' her mother asked. ''You aren't indentured. Any time you wish to withdraw from this arrangement, you simply repay Legate's expenses and leave.''

''I know,'' Anya said. She'd studied that clause and had checked it out with a lawyer who didn't anticipate a problem. Anya's payout from her husband's life insurance policies had left her with a substantial savings account to pay off any debts incurred to Legate.

In contrast to her mother, Slater was gently persuasive. ''Last night, you stayed at the cottage where you and Charlie will live. I'm sure you'll agree that it's large enough to accommodate a husband. In fact, Jeremy picked it out himself.''

It was obvious that Jeremy wanted this opportunity for their son. How could Anya say no?

Slater continued. ''If you marry and have other children, we'll make arrangements for a larger house.''

The likelihood of Anya reproducing again was slim. She never would have gotten pregnant without the experimental fertilization procedures developed by Legate.

Her mother was right. Why waste time worrying about

an improbable future? The important thing—right now—
was to provide the very best for Charlie.

She walked to the desk and picked up the pen. Her gaze
scanned the tightly written pages. She'd read them so many
times that the words were memorized. Why was she so
reluctant to sign this contract?

"Perhaps," Slater said, "you're worried about how
you'll spend your time while Charlie is in school."

The thought had crossed her mind. "I thought I might
find a teaching position in the area."

"Allow me to make you an offer," he said with a wide,
benevolent smile. "I'm familiar with your credentials in
linguistics."

Anya had conversational skills in dozens of dialects and
had taught high school Spanish, French and Japanese as
well as doing translations. "So you have a job for me?"

"Legate is an international operation. We have a regular
need for translators. Full-time and part-time."

"I accept."

She'd have employment. Charlie would have playmates
and a fantastic education. The facilities here were outstand-
ing. The cottage was charming. It seemed too good to be
true.

Anya lowered the pen to the paper and signed all three
copies of the contract.

AT THE CIRCULAR DRIVEWAY in front of the Legate mansion, Roman guided his silver Mercedes-Benz into his parking space near the entrance. The drive from the airport had
done nothing to lessen his frustration. He charged across
the flagstones. It was no coincidence that a supposed
emergency occurred in Los Angeles at the same moment
Anya and Charlie arrived in San Francisco. Slater had

manufactured that excuse; he meant to keep Roman away from Anya.

Had she signed the contract? There was no way Roman had been able to warn her of the dangers—not without blowing his cover and jeopardizing his investigation.

In the lavish foyer of the mansion, he approached the antique desk that was headquarters for Jane Coopersmith— possibly the only receptionist in the world with a photographic memory.

"Good afternoon, Jane."

Peering up at him through goggle-size eyeglasses, she gave a curt nod. "Roman."

She presented him with several little message notes, held between her thumb and forefinger. On top was one from Dr. Neville, head of the Legate psychiatric division, marked "Urgent" and underlined three times. Too bad. Neville would have to wait.

"Where can I find Mrs. Parrish and her son?"

Without consulting notes, she said, "Stables."

Not a conversationalist, Jane observed and recorded information more efficiently than any computer. But Roman didn't make the mistake of treating her like a machine. His smile was warm enough to melt butter. "You've always got the answer, Jane. What would this place be without you?"

"Chaos," she said with a slight thaw.

He exited through the rear of the mansion, passing the employee dining area where the remains of a catered buffet lunch were being cleared.

Whenever Roman was on the grounds, he assumed he was under surveillance. Like everyone else, his phones were bugged and his computer was monitored. The Legate security system made the Pentagon seem lax. Of course, precautions were necessary; Legate dealt with a lot of top secret projects for the U.S. government and other regimes worldwide. However, the intensity of the surveillance was due to Slater's need to control every detail. Anything and everything was reported to him. Nobody sneezed without Slater receiving an alert.

When Roman was here, his guard was up. It was vital that he maintain the illusion of being a loyal administrator. But it made life damned inconvenient.

Though he'd contacted Anya, he hadn't been able to honestly discuss the proposed contract with her. Even if they had been able to talk on a secure basis, he couldn't provide factual evidence that Legate was up to no good. To all appearances, the contract was a great opportunity for Charlie. But Roman's instincts told him it was wrong for her to be here.

He hurried past the maze toward the stables. Then he saw her. Astride a dappled mare, Anya rode at the edge of the trees. Her long, silky blond hair swirled in the breeze, and she was laughing—more carefree than he'd seen her since Jeremy's death.

Riding at a gentle pace, she held Charlie in front of her on the saddle. The mother and son were beautiful together. The boy's hair was a darker blond and his eyes were gray, but he was clearly a part of her. Roman felt an aching need to gather them both in his arms and carry them away from here, away from all these damned intrigues.

She saw him and waved, guiding the horse expertly toward him. As they approached, Charlie bounced in the saddle, talking a blue streak. "Hi, Roman. We're here, and I'm going to learn how to ride all by myself. This horse is Peggy for Pegasus, but she doesn't really know how to fly."

Anya reined the mare to a stop beside him. The smallish

palomino was well trained and groomed to perfection. Everything at Legate was first-class.

Charlie dived off the saddle into Roman's arms. "Make me a helicopter," Charlie demanded.

Roman lifted him high and twirled him around in circles before placing him on the ground.

With a giggle, Charlie shook off his dizziness and said, "We're going to live here."

"Are you?"

"I'm going to learn how to build my own helicopter and other stuff, too. And then…"

As Charlie continued to chatter, Roman looked up at Anya. Silhouetted against the sky, her eyes were a breathtaking blue. The exertion of their horseback ride flushed her cheeks. Erect in the saddle, she was tall, long-legged and fantastic.

Gracefully, she dismounted. Holding the bridle, she gave Roman a one-armed hug that was altogether unsatisfying. He wanted to feel her body molded against his, to stroke her slender shoulders and the curve of her waist.

"I decided," she said. "I signed the contract."

He nodded, wishing he could tell her she'd done the right thing. "There wasn't any other choice."

"And I'm going to be working here as a translator. I guess that means you're my boss."

An interesting twist. Slater must have realized that Anya would be bored without employment. Plus, if she worked here, Legate had even more control of her life. "I should warn you that I'm *very* demanding."

"No problem." Her nose crinkled as she grinned. "I'm *very* good."

Charlie bounced up beside them. "Put me back on Peggy. I want to ride some more."

"Whoa, Charlie," Anya chided. "Even cowboys are polite."

"Please, Roman," he said. "I want to ride more."

He lifted the boy into the saddle. "It's hard to keep your balance so you hold on to this thing right here. It's called a pommel."

"Got it," Charlie said. "Let's go, cowpoke."

Roman brought the reins around to the front to lead the mare back toward the stable. He glanced back over his shoulder toward the microwave dishes installed above an outbuilding. Every word of their conversation could be picked up. Surveillance cameras from three different angles might be watching.

Anya strolled beside him. "This arrangement is going to be perfect. I don't know why I hesitated so long before signing the contract."

"It's a big change, moving from your home in Denver."

"I've moved before. Often. I went to four, no, five different high schools. We had to go where Mother's consulting work took us."

"How is Claudette?" Roman didn't like Anya's mother. She was as cold as an ice cube, the very opposite of her emotion-driven daughter.

"Mother rented a house across the bay. I guess she's planning to stay in San Francisco for a while."

"To be close to you and Charlie."

"Seems odd." She gave a tight laugh. "Claudette isn't exactly the doting type."

"Not a cookie-baking grandma?"

"No way. I don't think she's ever even read a fairy tale, much less believed in one."

"But you do."

"Yup." She tossed her head, sending a ripple though her hair. The sunlight picked out strands of pure platinum. "I believe in fairy tales. No matter what else happens, there's got to be a happy ending.''

Though her words sounded simplistic, he heard determination in her voice. She was willing to fight for her happily-ever-after.

''Maybe here,'' she said. ''Maybe Legate is what I've been looking for all my life.''

He didn't want to encourage that fragile hope. There were too many signs to the contrary. In fairy-tale terms, Legate was the evil kingdom, ruled by an ogre named Slater. ''I understand that you'll have a cottage on the premises.''

''It's adorable. All furnished.'' Anya glanced up at him, looking for answers he couldn't give. ''I keep thinking it was weird that Jeremy never mentioned this plan to me. He had all these details in his will.''

Roman wasn't even sure Jeremy's will was valid; it had been prepared by the Legate legal staff. ''He never discussed it with me, either.''

''Weird,'' she repeated. ''I mean, Jeremy and I spent two weeks talking about what kind of sofa we should get. Then he makes this huge, life-altering plan without a blink in my direction.''

''It's not totally out of character,'' he reminded her. ''Once, Jeremy bought a car without even a test drive.''

''Because he liked the hood ornament.''

''He was capable of snap judgments.''

''That's true,'' she said. ''The new will was dated only a few weeks before his death, and he probably meant to discuss it when he came back to Denver.''

When she talked about Jeremy, the blue of her eyes grew dim. Her shoulders caved slightly. She was still grieving, and it troubled Roman to see her suffer. Her husband shouldn't have died. If Roman had been smarter, he might have prevented the tragedy.

He believed that the explosion at Building Fourteen had been rigged, but he still didn't know why. Why would Slater kill four scientists who worked for him? They were good employees—productive and nonconfrontational. Why did they have to die? After eight months of digging into the various global projects these scientists were working on, Roman still didn't have the answer.

"It's good to see you," Anya said.

"And you," he said. "You've put on weight."

"Excuse me?"

"That's a compliment." After Jeremy's death, she'd been skinny as a rail, unable to eat. "You look healthy."

"Healthy? Like a prize cow?" Her eyebrows arched. "If that's your standard pick-up line, you're going to be a bachelor forever."

"That wasn't even close to a pick-up line."

"And why not? We might be friends, but I'm still a single female. According to your reputation, you should be charming me off my feet."

"You're not an ordinary female." She was another man's wife. Even now, with Jeremy dead, she was still married to his memory.

From atop the horse, Charlie called out, "Mommy, look. I'm riding with no hands."

"Hold on to the pommel," she said. "Or you're getting off, mister."

"I want to go faster. Please."

"This is your first time on a horse," she said. "Take it easy."

"Okay, Mom."

She returned her attention to Roman, picking up their

conversation where it left off. "All right, Bachelor Number One, give me a real compliment. I need one."

For years, he'd tried not to think of Anya as an eligible woman. But she'd asked for it.

His guard went down. The facade of civility slipped away. He allowed his unspoken desires to rise to the surface. These thoughts had been simmering at the back of his mind from the first day he met her.

With smoldering eyes, he gazed into her heart-shaped face. His voice lowered to a seductive murmur, and he said, "When I see you here in the sunlight, with the wind in your hair and your lips as soft as rose petals, I know what miracles are. This vision of you is precious. I'll carry it with me forever."

"Oh." She gaped.

He relished the effect he had upon her, and he pressed his advantage, tenderly grasping her hand and lifting it to his lips to blow a light kiss across her knuckles. "You touch my heart."

"Oh, my."

"Anya, please. Let me touch you."

"Wow! You're good." She grabbed her hand back from him and fanned her face with it. "No wonder you have thousands of babes swooning all over you."

He looked away from her and started walking again. Though this flirting was a game, he'd meant every word. He wanted to touch her, to kiss her mouth, to make love to her.

They neared the stables where Anya's mother and Fredrick Slater stood waiting. The sight of Slater had the effect of a cold shower on Roman. He sloughed off his sensuality, any sign of vulnerability. Instead, he visualized himself as forged steel.

"There they are," Anya said. "Claudette and Slater. They almost look like a couple, don't they?"

Well matched in ruthless intelligence and ambition, they could have been MacBeth and his lady. "Almost."

"Roman, with this contract, am I doing the right thing?"

"It'll all work out." He wouldn't let anything bad happen to her or to Charlie.

At the stables, Slater wasted no time in pulling him to one side. "Did you handle the problem in Los Angeles?"

"It was nothing," Roman said. "A simple miscommunication."

"I suppose Anya told you that she and Charlie will be living here."

"Yes." He slipped on a pair of dark glasses, concerned that his eyes might betray his hostility.

"She seems a bit uncomfortable," Slater said. "That's not good for Charlie's transition. He needs to feel that Legate is his home. It's important for his mother to transmit that acceptance."

"According to whom?"

"Dr. Neville, the psychiatrist."

"I have an urgent message to contact him," Roman said.

"Yes, I know."

Slater's hands were clasped behind his back. In his tweed suit with his neat gray hair, he looked like the lord of the manor, out for a stroll on his magnificent grounds.

Roman lengthened his stride. He was a good six inches taller and wanted to make Slater stretch to keep up with him.

But the old man sensed what he was doing and halted. When he looked up, he probed with his gaze, taking Roman's measure with quick, stabbing glances. Slater wanted something. "You have a bond with Charlie's mother."

"I've known Anya for years."

"She's done a good job raising the boy. Neville said it was important to leave Charlie with his mother until he was five and had established a healthy bond."

"Then what?"

"Education, of course. Expanding the child's frame of reference."

Slater's analysis made it sound like he was talking about an experiment. Roman tried to match his detachment. "Exactly what are your goals with Charlie?"

"To nurture and develop his intelligence. At the same time, he must be a well-rounded individual. Too many of our geniuses are antisocial. Charlie will be high-functioning on many levels—theoretical, creative, even political. He might even become President of the United States."

Did Slater really think he could build his own president? Throw together the proper genetics for intelligence, add training and stir? This plan sounded like the insane ravings of a twenty-first-century Frankenstein.

"That boy," Slater said, "will be my legacy."

His legacy? But Slater wasn't the child's father or grandfather.

"I need your help, Roman."

"How?"

"While Charlie is settling into the program, I want his mother to be happy. I want her to feel she made the right decision in coming here. See to it."

"Could you be more specific?"

"She needs a man," Slater said.

Roman couldn't believe his ears. This crafty old bastard was ordering him to do the very thing he had wanted for years. Slater wanted him to become Anya's lover.

Chapter Two

At seven o'clock that evening Roman connected with Maureen, a slinky redhead. In her tight jeans and see-through blouse, she was hotter than wasabi on sushi. Not that her appearance mattered to him. Maureen wasn't a date. She was his contact inside the CIA, a special ops agent.

They met at a cheesy tavern in Oakland where the specialty of the house was tequila-fried perch, but they didn't need a menu. After a quick hello, they went to her car at the back of the parking lot, far from the neon sign above the entrance.

Maureen slid behind the steering wheel and turned on the radio. Instead of music, there was a whirring sound. "This interference noise disrupts any bugs or listening devices pointed in our direction."

"Nice tune," he said.

"You know how I love my secret-agent toys."

She'd been his contact for almost a year. When Roman learned that the think tank had manipulated federal regulations on offshore banking for an emerging Central American nation, he hooked up with a special branch of the CIA, and they assigned Maureen, an attractive woman who could easily pass as one of his dates. That was their cover.

"What's up?" she asked.

"I'm concerned about two innocent people who are now living on the Legate grounds. Anya Bouchard Parrish and her son, Charlie."

"She's the wife of your friend who was killed, right?"

He nodded. "Slater talked her into signing a contract that would allow him to raise and educate her son."

"Why?"

"Charlie has a genius IQ, and Slater wants to groom him. He thinks Charlie will be his legacy."

"But he's not related to the child?"

"No," Roman said.

In the dim glow from the dashboard, he saw her thoughtful frown. "I don't get it."

"Neither do I." But Roman had given the issue some thought. "Anya participated in a fertilization experiment at Legate. That was how she conceived her son. Slater might feel a proprietary connection."

"How does Mrs. Parrish feel about this?"

"She doesn't know." Roman frowned. None of this made sense. "By bringing her son to Legate, she thinks she's following her late husband's wishes."

"Why?"

"Jeremy made a provision in his will saying he wanted his son to attend the Legate school, starting when he was five."

"Do you believe he'd do that?"

"Not really," Roman said. "If his signature on the will is a forgery, how would I find out?"

"Get me the original. Our experts can verify."

That wouldn't be easy. He didn't want to alarm Anya by asking to see the document. "Even if the will was forged, it doesn't explain why Slater is so fixated on Charlie. True, the boy is smart, but there are plenty of whiz kids out there. Why Charlie?"

"Maybe there's a connection in Anya's family tree. Should we run a trace?"

"Not necessary." Anya's privacy had been invaded enough, and he knew just enough about her father to realize that an investigation could be a problem.

Maureen swept her thick auburn hair off her forehead and fastened it at her nape with a clip. Though her makeup was sultry, her attitude was all business. As always, when Roman allowed his gaze to wander over her body, he wondered where—in that tight-fitting outfit—she kept her gun.

"Bottom line," Maureen said. "Are these two people in danger?"

"Not Charlie. He'll be pampered like a prince."

"And his mother?"

He'd given Anya's safety a great deal of consideration and had decided there was no immediate peril. "She's safe for now. Slater won't let anything happen to her that might traumatize her son."

"So why did you contact me?"

"I wanted to give you a heads up," Roman said. "If it turns out that I'm wrong and Anya is threatened, I'm pulling the plug."

"Sorry to hear that. Your inside info has given us excellent leads."

"I'm not cut out for undercover work," he said. "I feel like crap when I'm encouraging somebody with one hand and betraying them with the other."

"Make no mistake," she said. "You're doing a good thing. Because of your information, we've been able to sever terrorist plots, stop an attempted takeover of the government in Burma and shut down an illegal munitions plant."

"For the greater good," he said in ironic reference to the Legate motto.

"It still amazes me," she said. "Who would have guessed that all those international bad guys consulted a think tank?"

"There's something else I need to tell you," he said. "In the future, you might not be the best person for me to contact."

Her pearly teeth flashed in the dark. "Does this mean you're breaking up with me?"

There had never been anything between them except for CIA business. "I can't be seen going on dates. My current assignment at Legate is to make Anya happy. You know, to romance her."

"Oh, ugh!" Right before his eyes, the hard-boiled CIA agent turned into a girly girl. Her voice rose an octave. "That's so creepy, Roman. How can you lead that poor woman on?"

"As if you've never used your physical assets to get what you wanted?"

"This doesn't sound like you." She peered through the dim dashboard light into his eyes. "You hate deception."

He returned her gaze. "Anya won't be hurt."

"How can you say that? You're planning to lead her down the garden path, to promise her a rose garden, to—"

"I won't lie to her," Roman said. "Anya will not be hurt. Never again."

"Oh, my God." Maureen gasped and leaned back in her seat. "You really care about this woman."

She had no idea how much he cared.

AT CHARLIE'S BEDSIDE, Anya leaned down to kiss her son's forehead. He was sound asleep at nine o'clock—a bit early, but this had been a hectic day. "Sleep well, sweetpea."

If he'd been awake, he might have complained about the

nickname. But now her son was quiet, breathing steadily, innocent as a little blond angel. She tucked the covers around his shoulders, closed the door to his bedroom and went downstairs.

This part of the day was Anya's alone time when she could reflect. For the past month, her private deliberations had focused on one thing: Should she or shouldn't she sign the contract?

Finally, that decision-making process was over. The ink on the document was dry, and it seemed that she'd done the right thing for Charlie. But why did her heart feel so heavy?

She stood in the center of the living room and slowly turned in a circle. The cottage wasn't exactly the way she would have decorated, but close. The earth-tone furniture was better quality than her own sofa and chairs in Denver. The bland artwork on the wall didn't appeal to her, but she loved the wall of bookshelves separating the living room and a modern kitchen with shiny new appliances.

She couldn't complain about the living accommodations. This cottage—which was equal to the square footage of her rented house in Denver—was cozy and comfortable. And free.

Slowly, she turned again. Her gaze flitted from the plasma-screen television hanging on the wall to the charming stone fireplace to the welcoming fruit basket on the side table. This wasn't the life she'd imagined for herself. It felt…too organized.

Anya wanted more adventure. An impulsive weekend vacation. A surprise visit from friends. And she doubted that unplanned excitement was included in the Legate program. *Spontaneous* would only be a word on Charlie's vocabulary list.

Might as well make the best of it. She padded around

the main floor, turning off the lamps, leaving one burning in case Charlie got up during the night and wandered. At the door to the cottage, she doused the porch light and stepped outside into the darkness. The cottage was surrounded by a forest of landscaping, giving the impression of seclusion. She couldn't see the gray stone mansion from here, but one of the outbuildings was only twenty yards away from her roofed porch that stretched the length of the cottage.

It was a beautiful night. The autumn breeze held a chill that stimulated her senses. She cinched the sash on her flannel robe more tightly and inhaled. The air was moist with a woodsy scent of cedar and pine. If she stood very still, she could hear the faint echo of the bay surf.

At the edge of the trees, she noticed movement from something much larger than a squirrel. "Who's there?"

A man stepped away from the shadows. "Good evening, ma'am."

She shouldn't be surprised. There were several other people who lived on these grounds. "Hello. Have we met?"

"No, ma'am."

As he came closer, she saw the dark blue uniform worn by Legate's security corps. His trousers were tucked into his boots, military-style. There was a holster attached to his belt, and he carried something else, held tight to his side.

"My name is Anya," she said.

"Yes, ma'am. I know."

"And you are?"

"Harrison," he said.

Staying on the porch, she edged closer to him. "Are you armed, Harrison?"

In answer, he revealed the object he'd been hiding. An automatic rifle.

She was shocked and more than a little upset. "Why do you have that gun?"

"Intruders." He took two steps back, fading again into the shadows. "Sorry to disturb you, ma'am."

Of course, she knew that Legate handled sensitive political and scientific information. Security was necessary, but she hadn't expected constant patrolling by armed guards.

Why was it necessary to have such intense protection? Harrison the security man looked like he was prepared to take on an army. What kind of place was she living in? The bracing chill turned icy cold, sinking deep through her flesh to her bones.

Back inside, she locked the doors. Sleep was out of the question. Anya whipped through the house, turning on the lights she'd extinguished only moments ago. My God, she'd made a terrible mistake. They couldn't live here. Not with an armed guard patrolling outside her front door!

When the telephone rang, she nearly jumped out of her skin. She grabbed the receiver. "Hello?"

"It's Roman. How are you doing?"

"Why is the security man carrying an Uzi?" she demanded.

"It's not an Uzi," he said. "His weapon is specially designed—"

"I don't care," she said. "How dangerous is this place? What kind of intruders are they expecting?"

"I'm over at the mansion, Anya. If you'd like, I can be at the cottage in three minutes."

"Hurry."

She slammed the phone into the cradle and went to the front window to watch for Roman's approach. He should have warned her. He never should have allowed her to bring Charlie into danger.

In the glow from the porch light, she saw Roman jogging

along the path toward the cottage. He'd changed from the suit he was wearing earlier into Levi's and a black leather jacket that made him look a bit dangerous himself. Dark and mysterious, Roman was a big man, over six feet tall and muscular.

Before he could knock, she opened the front door and placed her forefinger across her lips. "Shh. Charlie's sleeping."

"Are you all right?"

"I'm a little freaked," she said.

When he stepped inside, his male energy filled the house. She could have sworn that the lightbulbs burned a little brighter and that the temperature rose several degrees. He placed his hands on her shoulders and stared down into her eyes. In a husky whisper, he asked, "What happened?"

"I stepped outside for some air and met a security man who was armed like a commando. Why is he here?"

"This is an international think tank. We handle sensitive, top secret projects—scientific and political. The guards are a precaution."

"Against what? Terrorists? Did I bring my son into a war zone?"

His smile was warm and reassuring. He lightly brushed her hair back from her forehead, and she remembered his gentleness—unusual for such a big man. "You're safe here."

How could he say that? Her husband died here. Of course, that was an accident, unrelated to the security corps. "If Charlie sees armed guards, he'll be scared."

"I doubt that," he said. "Your son might be a genius, but he's also a typical boy. He'll think the guns are cool."

"That's worse! I don't want him to be comfortable around weapons." Her fingers clenched into fists, ready to battle an invisible enemy. "I might be overreacting."

"Maybe."

He lifted her chin so she had to look directly into his face. "What's really bothering you?"

"I don't know."

As she continued to gaze up at him, she became distracted. An errant strand of his thick, black hair fell across his forehead. His deep-set eyes shone with a dark compelling light. Up close, his irises weren't completely black, but a dark tawny-brown. His firm jawline was outlined with a day's growth of stubble.

She focused on his well-shaped mouth. His smiling lips were the most welcoming feature in that hard chiseled face. *What would it be like to kiss those lips?*

Immediately, she squelched that impetuous idea. Roman had a reputation as a ladies' man. He dated models and socialites. He lived in a bachelor's pad on a cliffside—a legendary setting for seduction. Even if he had been a suitable person to kiss, she wasn't ready to go down that path. It had only been eight months....

She caught hold of his hands and lowered them from her shoulders. Roman was a friend. She wouldn't allow herself to think of him in any other way. "Would you like some tea?"

"I'd rather have wine."

"Me, too." She tossed her head, trying to shake the idea of Roman as a man she could be attracted to. "But I don't know if I have wine."

"Allow me."

He led the way into the kitchen where he opened a cabinet near the back door. The face of the cabinet door was oak, like the rest of the cabinetry, but it sealed like a refrigerator. Inside was a full wine rack.

"White or red?" he asked.

"Merlot," she said. "Is that another refrigerator?"

"A mini wine cellar. It's sealed to keep the temperature stable at the proper fifty-five degrees with humidity of seventy percent." He pulled out a corked bottle. "We take our wine seriously in Northern California."

He went to the cabinets above the sink and found two stemmed wineglasses. Quite obviously, Roman knew his way around this kitchen far better than she did. "You've been here before."

"We've used this place as a guest cottage," he said. "But it's yours now. Everything in here is yours."

So she'd been told, but Anya couldn't help feeling like she was at a fancy resort with an honor bar that she'd somehow end up paying for. "A nice young man from the public relations department showed me around. From what he said, I don't even have to go to the market. I just check off the items I want on a list. My order is delivered to the doorstep."

Using a corkscrew, Roman opened the bottle. "Before you stock up on food, I suggest you try the lunch and dinner buffets in the mansion. The chef is *cordon bleu.*"

"Are you saying he's a better cook than I am?"

He grinned. "I've had your spaghetti, Anya."

She remembered a disastrous dinner she prepared while Roman was in Denver after the funeral. Thinking that it would be good for her to return to her regular routine, she put together the ingredients for homemade spaghetti sauce. Then her brain shut down. The sauce bubbled too long on high flame, and the result was charred. "Dinner isn't only about food," she said. "It's a time for talk and catching up on the day."

"A private time for you and Charlie," he said.

"We're going to need some space and privacy," she said, accepting the wineglass he held toward her. "This educational program is so packed with activity that he'll need a chance to wind down."

He peered across the rim of his glass, making eye contact. "Be careful, Anya."

She tried to match his steady gaze, but she wasn't that bold. Her glance slipped to the floor. "Why should I be careful?"

"Don't spend so much time worrying about Charlie that you ignore your own needs."

She took a sip. The light merlot slid easily down her throat, leaving a pleasant aftertaste. "My own needs, eh? Well, that's all I've been thinking about tonight. I'm afraid I'll feel trapped here. That I won't have..."

"Won't have what?" he asked.

"Fun. That I won't have any fun." She rolled her eyes and tasted her wine again. "It sounds foolish when I say it out loud. I'm an adult. A widow. Why should I be concerned with fun and games?"

"Let me guess," he said. "Because you never had much fun when you were growing up."

"My mother did a good job raising me." She automatically defended Claudette. Her mother had been a single parent with a demanding job. "She didn't have a lot of time for me. Her skills were in demand, and we traveled all over the place. East Coast, West Coast and in between. Plus we lived abroad. Pacific Rim. Africa. Europe."

"Was it fun?" he asked.

"Not for me," she admitted.

It seemed odd that they'd never really talked about her early life before. During the days she spent with Roman after the funeral, they talked about Jeremy. Or about Charlie. Or they just sat together, staring into the middistance between real life and tragedy.

She took another deep sip. "It's bad enough being the

new girl in town. When everybody else speaks a foreign tongue, it's even worse.''

''You felt isolated,'' he said. ''Trapped.''

His snap analysis hit close to the truth. Being at Legate felt very much like her childhood when she had no control over what happened and was dragged along like an inconvenient piece of luggage. ''Am I so transparent?''

''Hell, no. You're an intelligent, complex woman.''

''I don't want to be complex.'' She carried her wine to the oak table in the dining area between the kitchen and living room and sat. Usually, Anya didn't drink alcoholic beverages, and the wine was already having an agreeable, relaxing effect. ''All I ever really wanted was a normal life. A normal family. A nice little house. A pleasant, low-pressure job. A garden. Maybe a golden retriever named Rover.''

''And when Jeremy died, you feel like you lost that chance.''

''I miss him,'' she said.

''So do I.''

When he sat beside her at the round table, she felt warm and settled, as if this were the way things ought to be. A man, a woman and her son upstairs asleep. Normal. ''Thanks for rushing over here.''

''Whenever you need me, I'll be around.''

She couldn't believe that promise. He might have the best intentions, but he also had a life. ''Baby-sitting me would cut into your social action.''

He shrugged.

''I've heard all about your infamous bachelor pad,'' she said. ''A chamber of seduction?''

''You can see for yourself. Come to dinner on Friday night.''

"I don't think so," she said quickly. "I don't want to leave Charlie with a baby-sitter so soon."

"Bring him," Roman said.

Dubious, she toyed with her merlot, swirling the rose-colored liquid in her glass. "I'm not going to have to explain to him about mirrors over the bed or anything, am I?"

"It's not the Playboy mansion," he assured her.

Part of her wished that his place really was a splendid, sensual pleasure palace. What would it be like to have this very good-looking man sweep her off her feet and into his bedroom?

This time, her sip of wine was a huge, sloshing gulp. She needed liquid to douse these inappropriate flickers of desire. Once again, her gaze came to rest upon his lips, moistened with sweet merlot.

Why on earth would she think that a notorious bachelor like Roman Alexander would be interested in her? Here she sat in her ancient flannel robe and fuzzy slippers. No makeup. Her hair hung uncombed around her cheeks. She certainly wasn't the picture of desirability.

Yet he communicated a sexual energy. She felt it in the way he looked at her, the arch of his eyebrow, the way he lifted his wineglass to his lips. When he spoke, his rich baritone struck a trembling chord within her. Likewise, his silences were full of portent and promise.

She blurted, "Do you think I'll ever get married again?"

He reached across the table and placed his large hand atop hers. His flesh was warm. His touch? Pure sensuality. "Yes, Anya. You'll find love again."

It was the answer she wanted to hear. Earlier, she dared not even ask herself that question, but that was exactly what had been bothering her. Not the armed guard outside the door. Not a lack of fun. She wanted to know if love was an option in her future.

"Friday night," she said. "We'll be there. Me and Charlie."

"It's a date."

Maybe not a date in the single woman's sense of the word, but it was enough for right now.

Chapter Three

The next morning, Roman arrived at Legate early. He needed some heavy-duty exercise before his eight-o'clock breakfast meeting. He hadn't slept well. After he spent a full night of tossing and turning, his bedsheets were as tangled as his emotional response to Anya Bouchard Parrish.

Leaving his Mercedes in the parking lot, he strode to the asphalt path and did a quick warm-up. The weather was relatively clear, and the dawn mist was colored a soft pink—the color of Anya's lips. There was a nip in the air, but he'd chosen to wear only nylon shorts and a long-sleeved T-shirt. He wanted the reality of a cold wind against his bare legs.

He started at a jog on the path that circled the mansion. Yesterday, Fredrick Slater had asked him to make Anya happy. Anything Slater suggested was likely to come with a multilevel ulterior motive. But Roman was only too glad to comply with this request. He couldn't stop thinking about her, imagining what it would be like to taste that lovely mouth and tangle his fingers in her silky blond hair.

At the same time, he felt guilty. In his mind, she was still Jeremy's wife. She still wore the wedding band Jeremy had placed on her finger for better or much, much worse.

His death wounded her deeply...which meant she was vulnerable. Roman didn't want to take advantage of her.

He picked up the pace, aware that he was nearing Anya's cottage. Through the shrubbery, he could see a second floor window that might be her bedroom. He stared at the white window frame outlined against the slate-blue house. The curtains were drawn. Was she sleeping? He envisioned her delicate body beneath the sheets. She'd roll to her side, and the sheet would slip lower on her breasts. His fingers itched to touch her, to caress the soft white skin on her inner thigh. When he kissed her, she would smell of honeysuckle.

Running harder, he proceeded to the winding stairs that led down to the beachfront. After eighty-seven steps down the cliffside, his custom-made running shoes hit the hard-packed sand on the narrow beach. This portion of his morning run was his favorite. At the edge of the bayside surf, he paused. He bobbed his head and shoulders, loosening up. After a few stretches, he shook out the muscles in his legs, then dropped into a crouch. *Ready, set, go.*

His toes dug into the sand as he went into a full-out sprint—a dash at the water's edge. He ran hard. Ice-cold droplets splashed onto his calves. The morning mist parted before him. Gulls and a flock of sandpipers took wing. His pulse accelerated. A rush of adrenaline shot through his veins.

At the rugged black rocks that marked the edge of this private beach, he stopped. Breathing hard, he bent double.

When he lifted his head, he saw a tall man in a three-piece gray suit coming toward him. Dr. Lowell Neville, head of Legate's psychiatric division. Damn it, Roman didn't want to talk to him.

"I expected to find you here," Neville called out.

"If you don't mind, I'd like to finish my run."

"I mind," Neville said crisply. "You ignored my messages from yesterday."

"I was busy," Roman said.

"Yet you found time to contact the charming Mrs. Parrish. Even to visit her cottage last night."

"That was Slater's order. He asked me to make sure Anya was comfortable." Roman paced in a tight circle. "Sorry, Doc. I need to keep moving or I'll stiffen up. We'll have to talk later."

"This is about your former assistant."

"Peter Bunch." An overqualified young man with a bright future, he'd quit two weeks ago. "What about him?"

Neville planted himself in Roman's path, forcing his attention. "Peter Bunch is missing."

The wind left Roman's lungs. "Missing?"

"As in 'missing person,'" Neville said. "The police were here, asking questions."

Roman caught a gulp of air. *Damn it!* Did Peter's disappearance have something to do with his employment at Legate? Purposely, Roman dropped his gaze to the sand beneath his feet, not wanting to betray his suspicions to a trained psychiatric observer. Especially not to Neville. The company shrink was Slater's toady. "I'm sorry to hear about Peter."

"How was your relationship with him? When he quit, did he express hostility toward Legate?"

"He left because he was invited to join an archaeological expedition in South America. He had a master's degree in archaeology. Working in the field was more to his liking than running errands for me."

"Did you have any reason to believe Peter would betray you?"

"Our personal relationship was fine."

Roman lifted his gaze and focused on Neville. The psychiatrist's thick black eyebrows contrasted his short-trimmed white hair and mustache. He was a fastidious man, always dressed in a suit with a conservative silk necktie and matching pocket handkerchief. His lips barely moved as he said, "You can be a hard person to work for."

"What's that supposed to mean?"

"What do you think it means?" Neville arched his left eyebrow.

"I've got no clue," Roman said.

"It occurs to me that your assistant would have access to confidential information. If he held a grudge against you, he might have attempted to sell this data. Would you have any knowledge of—"

"No." Roman spoke with a cold finality. He didn't want Neville trotting down this path.

"Well, I certainly hope Peter's greed hasn't led to unfortunate circumstances."

"Like what?" Roman said. "Do you think he was hurt? Murdered?"

"And why would you draw that conclusion?"

"Because I'm one hell of a fatalist." Roman started across the sand to the stairs, then turned and jogged backward. "Why did it occur to you that Peter might be selling Legate secrets?"

"Isn't it obvious?" Neville sneered. "We have a leak."

Roman turned away and jogged toward the stairway that climbed the steep cliff. He hoped with all his heart that nothing bad had happened to Peter Bunch. Had he been selling secrets? Doubtful. And he couldn't possibly be the leak. That honor belonged to Roman alone. He inhaled a deep breath and took the stairs two at a time.

ON HER FOURTH DAY at Legate, Anya had a bad case of the fidgets. While doing her translating work in a library cubicle on the first floor of the mansion, she checked her wristwatch dozens of times, marking the passage of each separate minute.

Today was Friday. Tonight was her dinner with Roman. At two in the afternoon, her part-time work was over, and she strolled back to the cottage with nowhere else to go and nothing else to do. Not tired enough for a nap. Not energetic enough to start a project. As she sorted through the clothing in her closet, deciding what to wear, she felt a rising sense of anticipation. "I haven't gone anywhere in four days." As soon as the words left her lips, she frowned. Talking to herself? Not a good sign.

At four-thirty, Charlie burst through the front door. "Mommy, do you know what a polymer is? A whole bunch of molecules. That's chemistry."

"Right," she said.

"We made a really stinky polymer today. Next week, we're going to build rockets and send stink bombs to Mars."

She leaned back in the rocking chair in the front room and listened to her son talk. His bubbling conversation gladdened her heart. She was pleased that Charlie wanted to share everything with her. Tomorrow was Saturday, and she'd have him all to herself. "Hey, sweetpea," she interrupted.

"Jeez, Mom. Don't call me that."

"We're going to Roman's house for dinner. He'll be picking us up in about half an hour. You ought to wash up before we go."

"Okay."

No sooner had he hiked up the staircase than there was a knock at the door. Roman was early. Already here.

When she opened the door, she stared for a moment. Roman really was gorgeous, much too sexy for his own good. His black hair was slightly mussed. His tawny-brown eyes shone with a warm luster, and his grin hinted at seduction. He wore a pin-striped charcoal suit with no necktie. The collar of his white shirt was open. In his hand he held a simple bouquet of white daisies. "For you."

"But we're going to your house," she said. "I should be the one bringing a gift."

"Having you there is gift enough," he said.

She recognized his tone. "That's your flirting voice. I remember when we were walking with Charlie's pony and you showed me how you knocked women off their feet."

"And?"

"Stop it," she ordered.

"Force of habit," he said. "When I saw you standing there in that little black dress, looking so beautiful, I forgot this wasn't a date."

"I don't have much of a selection on clothes. Most of my stuff is back in Denver." Since she hadn't wanted to leave Charlie here alone, her mother had returned to Denver to arrange for the move. Anya shrugged. "It was either the black dress or jeans."

"Don't apologize," he said. "You look perfect."

"Thank you." She enjoyed his compliments. Being around Roman reminded her that she was still a woman. She took the daisies and held the door wider so he could come inside. "And thank you for the flowers."

Charlie clattered down the stairs and leaped at Roman. "Helicopter," he demanded.

"Not indoors." But Roman lifted him up high. "Touch the ceiling, Charlie."

"Got it. We're going to your house."

"That's right." Roman set him down on the floor. "I've got something for you."

He reached into his pocket and produced a rectangular,

red lacquered box. "This is a Chinese puzzle box. You have to figure out the puzzle to get it open."

Anya returned to the front room after putting the daisies in a vase.

"Look, Mom!" Charlie held up the box. "It's from China."

"Chinatown," Roman corrected. "Just across the bay."

"We'll have to go there," Anya said. "As soon as my car gets here from Denver, we can take all kinds of trips."

"To the moon?" Charlie asked.

"Why not?" She laughed. "The moon and beyond."

They slipped into coats and went out the door, heading along the path to the parking lot. Anya felt like singing. She wasn't accustomed to being so sequestered. "It feels like I'm escaping the monastery."

"Legate has that effect," Roman said. "That's why I don't choose to live here."

"I can't imagine you as a monk. You're not exactly the sackcloth-and-ashes type."

"Plus I hate the haircut."

He opened the car door for her, and she slipped inside. A buttery leather interior wrapped around her. There were more dials on the dashboard than in a small aircraft. Nice car! But what else would she expect from Roman? He demanded the best of everything. Tailored clothes. Fine wine. Even his sneakers were custom-made. She could hardly imagine what his bay-front house looked like.

Anya turned to check on Charlie in the back seat. "Buckle up, young man."

"I'm going to solve this puzzle now," he informed her.

"Don't be so sure," Roman said as he closed his car door and plugged his key into the ignition. "Some people take days to solve a puzzle box."

"Not me," Charlie said.

"You think you're that smart?" Roman teased.

"For sure. Neville says I'm a genius."

"Neville?" Anya craned her neck to look at her son. "When did you talk to him?"

"I dunno." Charlie eyed his puzzle box. "Maybe yesterday."

Anya frowned. She didn't want the company psychiatrist examining her son. Not without her permission. "I bumped into Neville today. I'm surprised he didn't mention your visit."

Charlie didn't answer. He was absorbed in puzzle-solving.

"What do you think of Neville?" Roman asked.

She shrugged noncommittally, not wanting to say anything negative in front of Charlie. "He's very tidy."

"That's an understatement," Roman muttered. "The man alphabetizes the magazines on his coffee table."

Under her breath, she asked, "What's with his matching necktie and pocket hankie?"

"He has different colors for different days of the week. Blue on Monday. Red on Friday. That must be his day to get wild."

"Wild?" She tried to picture Dr. Neville in an orgy mood and failed. "I can't see it."

"But don't let his eccentricities fool you. Neville isn't somebody you want to mess with."

As they drove through the Legate gates, the atmosphere seemed to change. The pale blue sky expanded into a wider, brighter vista. Roman exhaled a deep breath. The tension lines across his forehead seemed to relax.

"TGIF," she said. "Your job must be pretty stressful."

"And how about you? How's the translating work?"

She could use a bit more stress. "Not exactly my dream job."

"You're bored."

He sounded so disappointed that she was tempted to lie and tell him everything was hunky-dory. But Anya had never been one to keep her true feelings to herself. "Bored stiff."

"Still looking for fun?"

"You bet."

"There's fun coming up pretty soon," he said. "Halloween. Everybody dresses up, and the kids from the school go trick-or-treating in the different departments."

Anya found it difficult to reconcile the intense research and scientific experimentation that was the primary focus of Legate with the activities in the school, even if all the kids were geniuses.

"Are you telling me that all these Nobel laureates put on silly masks?"

"They love the chance to goof off," he said. "In the meantime, we'll get you started on more complex translation assignments."

All she'd done thus far was proofread documents that were already translated by a computer service. "What kind of complex assignments?"

"The top secret stuff."

"You're joking."

"I'm not," he said. "We do geopolitical treatises and scientific experimentation on an international level. Jeremy worked on a couple of biochemical projects where the end results were reviewed by the President of the United States and Britain's Prime Minister."

"He never told me."

"Which is why it's called top secret."

It irritated her to imagine projects that Jeremy didn't tell her about. They were supposed to trust each other with everything. She'd thought their marriage was as open as sunshine. Instead, he'd been clandestine in his work. And in setting up the Legate schooling for Charlie. What else hadn't Jeremy told her about? The armed guards at Legate, she thought. The high walls surrounding the compound.

As they crossed a bridge, she called over her shoulder to Charlie. "Bridge. Pick up your feet and hold your breath for good luck."

"Not now, Mom. I'm busy."

"The Bay Area is full of bridges," Roman said. "Around here, you'll build up a stockpile of luck."

"Good." Because she had a sneaking feeling that she might need all the luck she could get.

THE ELDERLY CHINESE MAN gazed impassively through the windshield as he tailed the Mercedes at a discreet distance.

"Don't let them see us," his companion warned.

"I am always cautious, Wade. You have no cause for concern."

But Wade Bouchard couldn't help feeling tense. After all these years, they were finally close to attaining their ultimate goal, which was nothing less than the absolute destruction of the Legate Corporation.

Wade was part of SCAT, Scientists Concerned About Truth. He and his associates had dedicated their lives to fighting those who used pure science for unethical purposes. Most of their battles were a matter of public record, but SCAT was ready to further their aims by whatever methods were necessary, including theft and violence. Wade had taken a bullet for his cause. And he killed a man in Taiwan. The face of that poor soul still haunted his nightmares, but he'd do the same again. Some principles were more important than life or death.

He could only pray that Anya would not disrupt his current mission. She had to agree. She had to understand that it was the only way to redeem the boy. Charlie. Wade's grandson.

Chapter Four

Anya wasn't wildly impressed by her first view of Roman's house. Unremarkable landscaping obscured the front doorway and walls, which appeared to be little more than bland gray stucco. She noticed very few blooming flowers—not that autumn was the season for spectacular floral display.

When they parked inside the garage, Charlie gave a cheer. "I did it! I got the puzzle box open!"

"Good for you," she said.

"Look what's inside." In his hand, he held a tiny dragon. The jaws were wide open as if the dragon were laughing.

"It's for protection," Roman said. "Keep that dragon with you, and you'll always be safe from harm."

Charlie regarded the statuette solemnly, then he held it toward her. "You need this more than I do, Mom."

She was touched and, at the same time, concerned. "Why do you think I need protecting?"

"Duh," he said. "Because you're a girl."

"Girls can take care of themselves just as well as boys." It was never too early to start teaching tolerance; she didn't want to raise a little misogynist. "You keep the dragon. It's your special gift from Roman."

Charlie stuffed the statuette in his pocket, unfastened his seat belt and popped open the car door. "Let's go."

The garage led into the kitchen where track lighting illuminated stainless steel appliances and polished granite countertops. The lines were clean and efficient, but it wasn't until she stepped into the living area that Anya had the full dramatic impact of Roman's high-tech home. Two-story, plate-glass windows offered a breathtaking view of bay and sky. The interior walls were accented with sea-foam green and burgundy. Unusual colors, but they worked well with the chrome lamps and warm hardwood floors. Charlie dashed around the room, testing the modern, modular furniture.

She'd expected a sexy den of iniquity, but this wasn't it. "Very classy," she said. "Your home suits you."

"I'm almost scared to show you the upstairs."

With Charlie in the lead, they ascended an open staircase to the second level, which was one huge room. Up here, the predominant colors were eggshell-white and a hot, passionate red. At one end was a high-tech Plexiglas office space. In the center was a conversation area. At the far end, separated by a black lacquered Chinese screen, was a massive four-poster bed in black and chrome.

Aha! This was the bachelor pad, the sheik's boudoir. The rich, deep red bedcover and dozens of pillows hinted at lavish, seductive delights. Mesmerized, Anya drifted toward it. On the bedside table were three buttons.

"Go ahead," Roman said. "Push the buttons."

She glanced nervously toward her son. Was this something he should see?

The first button adjusted the vertical blinds on the wall-to-wall windows, allowing a view of the bay. That seemed innocent enough.

When she pressed the second button, the bed began to vibrate. She arched an eyebrow. "Back problems?"

"It also heats up," he said.

"I'll bet it does."

She turned it off and touched the third button. A wide-screen television rose from a chest at the foot of the bed.

"Wow!" Charlie clapped his hands. "I want a bed just like this when I grow up."

Anya gave a disapproving sniff. This was not a role model she wanted her son to emulate.

"This part of the room is better." Roman pointed Charlie toward his office and said, "Computer on."

The flat screen came to life, showing a crystal clear picture of an underwater coral reef. The computer spoke in a sultry female voice. "Welcome home, Roman. It's 5:32 in the afternoon."

Charlie ran up to the screen. "What else does she do?"

"Computer, music," Roman said. "Classical."

The room filled with the throbbing opening notes to Ravel's *Bolero*. The sound resonated from several hidden speakers. Incredible! Anya felt as if she were inside an orchestra pit.

"Computer, softer," Roman said.

The computer responded, lowering the volume.

"Can I talk to her?" Charlie asked.

"Sorry, buddy. She only responds to my voice."

Anya stepped up beside them. "Why are you guys referring to the computer as a female?"

"Jeez, Mom. Didn't you hear her voice? She's a girl."

And Anya wasn't sure she wanted her five-year-old son associating with this sexy-sounding machine. What else was this computer programmed to do?

"Computer, games," Roman said. A menu popped up on the screen. "What do you like to play, Charlie?"

"Acto-Dinosaurs." He wriggled with excitement. "And I get to be Caveman."

Roman typed in a few commands, accessing the program, which was one Legate had created. He placed Charlie in the chair in front of the screen and handed him a joystick. "Knock yourself out, kiddo. Your mom and I will be downstairs making dinner."

"Okay." Charlie was already absorbed in the game, lining up a series of battles with snarling cyberdinosaurs.

With one last speculative glance at the sumptuous bed, Anya followed Roman downstairs. "I'm impressed. Your house is fantastic."

"Glad you like it," he said. "It was already built, but I knocked out a couple of walls and opened it up. Made the top floor into one room."

"It turned out beautifully. How did you learn to do this design stuff?"

"Before I started working at Legate, I had a career in contracting. I did a lot of custom homes, but my preference was big buildings. High-rises. Skyscrapers."

"What made you decide to change careers?"

In the kitchen, he removed a foil-covered tray from the refrigerator. "It wasn't that big a switch. Contracting and development requires a lot of administrative work—scheduling, negotiating and budget. Legate offered me a wider arena."

She detected a note of sadness in his voice. "Do you miss contracting?"

"In a way. There's something satisfying about putting a plan down on paper and seeing it through to completion. At Legate, nothing is ever simple."

When he peeled back the foil, she caught a tantalizing whiff of a fragrant marinade drowning three steaks. "You never told me you could cook."

"Every bachelor has at least three things they can make. All of mine involve red meat." He handed her a bottle of red wine from the fridge. "Grab a couple of glasses from the shelf by the sink and come with me."

They went outside through a sliding glass door. A long deck stretched the entire length of the house. Built out from the cliff, the deck seemed suspended in air. Anya went to the railing and peered over the edge. The drop was thirty feet to a rocky shoreline where breakers splashed, throwing up a frothy spray. "Good thing I'm not afraid of heights."

"Or earthquakes," he said. "When I moved in, I had the supports redesigned to compensate for shifting earth and erosion. But if the Big One hits, this deck is toast."

"You like having a bit of danger in your life, living on the edge." She looked down. "Literally."

He fired up the gas grill and placed the steaks on it. "Neville calls it risk-aggressive behavior. For some reason, this is a positive attribute for a paper-pushing administrator."

"You don't strike me as a paper-pusher."

"You'd be surprised at how boring my life can be." With the steaks sizzling, he joined her at the railing and pointed to the west. "If we stand right here, we can watch the sun dip below the horizon."

The skies, frothed with clouds, had begun to take on a crimson tinge. A salty sea breeze brushed her cheeks and throat, but Anya was warm inside the black blazer she wore over her dress. She looked up at the broad-shouldered man who stood beside her. Now that she'd started digging below his polished surface, she wanted to know more.

"We've never talked much about you," she mused. "I know that you and Jeremy went to high school together in Denver. You were a runner."

"I still hold the school record for the 500." He smiled down at her. "I've always been fast."

"So I've heard." Jeremy had told her all sorts of wild stories about Roman and his harem, but she was beginning to see him as a multifaceted person who was far more fascinating than a mere womanizer. "I don't think I've ever heard you talk about your family."

"Probably not." He opened the wine and filled their glasses.

"Come on, Roman. Tell me about your mother and father."

"My mother was a Gypsy," he said, taking a sip. "That's why I'm named Roman, short for Romani. The Gypsy word for man."

Very appropriate. Roman was the quintessential man. Utterly virile. "Go on."

"Gypsies are supposed to be wanderers, and my mother was true to form. She took off for good when I was ten."

"I'm sorry," she said.

"Don't be. She was impossible and loud. Godawful loud. Always yelling about something. And my father wasn't much better. He stuck around for me and my younger brother, but he never was much good at making a living."

"Where is he now?"

"Don't know," Roman said. "Don't care."

"And your brother?"

"Lukas was killed in a motorcycle accident about ten years ago." A shadow darkened his features. "I miss him."

But he didn't keep photos. Roman wasn't a man who dwelled in the past. He took what life threw at him and moved on. Anya wished she could do the same. "My childhood was the opposite of yours. It was my father who left. In a way, we're mirror images of each other."

"Not really. Your mother was successful. You traveled

the globe. My family never left Denver, and we barely scraped by.''

Having money made a difference. It was true. And Anya's father hadn't completely deserted her. He stayed in touch with birthday cards, phone calls and the occasional visit.

She'd always thought her life would have been easier if he'd completely abandoned her. That way, he'd be gone for good, and she'd be able to forget all about him.

"About your father," Roman said. "I don't remember seeing him at the funeral."

"He telephoned." And he had sounded truly, deeply sympathetic. His voice was at the edge of tears. But he told her he couldn't be with her. His presence might bring danger.

This was the most perplexing aspect of her relationship with Wade Bouchard. He claimed to be part of an international cadre of scientists who were dedicated to bringing unethical practices and experiments to light. If she believed in his goals, her father was an admirable person. "Dad was always racing off to save the world. Like a superhero. Supposedly, he stayed away from me and my mother so we wouldn't be attacked by his enemies."

"He's in SCAT, isn't he? Scientists Concerned About Truth."

"I never understood that nebulous organization. Occasionally, they issue statements to the press or on the Internet. And they have a dinky little office in Washington. But a worldwide organization?" She shook her head. "It seems more likely that my dad is a raging paranoid—fighting demons that don't exist."

"Those sound like your mother's words."

Anya nodded. "Mother doesn't have many good things to say about Wade."

"For what it's worth," Roman said. "I don't think your father is delusional. There's ample room for ethical concerns when it comes to the business of science and technology."

"Of course. But there are also rational and legal methods for investigation."

"And if those methods fail?"

What was he suggesting? "You can always tell what's right from wrong."

"Can you?"

He returned to the grill to tend the steaks, leaving her at the railing. She stared out into space, lulled by the rhythmic wash of waves against the rocks below. She should have been peaceful, but a small voice teased at the edge of her consciousness. What's right? What's wrong?

She remembered the Legate motto—For The Greater Good. It suggested that the needs of the many were more important than the needs of the few. Logical? Yes, but not always true. Legate's policies had apparently resulted in enemies so dangerous that they needed armed security guards and high walls.

Amid all the bustling activity of genius at work, she had sensed the ominous undercurrents. Nothing she could precisely define. Just a feeling. A certain tension. She sipped her wine. On the grounds of Legate, her husband had died a violent death. Was the explosion at Building Fourteen really an accident?

A shudder went through her. Beneath her jacket, she felt a chill that had nothing to do with the weather. "When you referred to unethical practices, were you talking about Legate?"

"I'd rather not talk about Legate. It's the weekend. Time to relax."

But she couldn't let this go. "Have I brought my son into a potentially dangerous situation?"

He met her gaze directly but didn't speak. The fading sunlight cast intriguing shadows across his face, highlighting his high cheekbones. A man of Gypsy blood, he was exotic, and at the same time, strong and stable as a rock. Utterly unreadable. There were secrets locked inside him. That was all she could tell for sure.

Reaching toward her, he lightly brushed a lock of hair off her forehead. "You'll be safe. I'll take care of you and Charlie. I'll be your personal good luck dragon."

His baritone harmonized with the wind and surf. The tones were deeply soothing. She wanted to believe him, to trust in the warmth she felt when he was near.

He leaned toward her. His intentions were clear; he meant to kiss her. She ought to object, but his closeness seemed like a good thing…a very good thing. She wanted a kiss. For reassurance. Her head tilted back. Her eyelids blinked shut.

His lips were firm. His mouth exerted a pressure that demanded a response, and she surprised herself by kissing him back.

Pure sensuality flooded her body, sending heat through her veins, lifting her off her feet as though she were floating on a cloud. It was only a kiss but felt like more. A promise of future passion and fulfillment.

Standing here at the edge of the world, she reveled in the whisper of the surf, the tang of the breeze, the taste of this man who she'd been acquainted with for years…and had never really known. Until now.

"Mommy?"

She turned. Charlie stood inside the house, behind the sliding glass door. His wide gray eyes accused her.

Instinctively, she reached toward him. Her wine spilled, and she dropped her glass. It shattered at her feet.

Chapter Five

Roman couldn't sleep. He threw aside the covers on his bed and rose from the black satin sheets. Naked, he paced soundlessly across the thick carpet on his bedroom floor. The glow of moonlight through the windows faintly illuminated the bed, the sitting area and the desk. His bare feet traced a figure eight in front of the windows.

It was unfortunate that Charlie had caught them in a kiss. The boy wasn't ready for anybody to take his father's place, and he was jealous of his mother's attention. Throughout their dinner, the five-year-old had clung to Anya's side like a limpet, which caused her to be uncomfortable and tense.

And Roman felt the same. He shouldn't have kissed her, no matter how much he wanted to. It was too soon. Damn it! He prided himself on self-control, and he was losing it.

He couldn't decide what to do. What was right? What was wrong?

Should he tell Anya about his undercover work? She'd been on target when she guessed that Legate was unethical. But if she knew the extent of Slater's treachery, she'd bolt. And Roman wasn't sure the timing was right for her to leave Legate.

This was all about Charlie. Slater wanted the boy to stay with him, and he was ruthless in getting what he wanted.

If Anya was in his way, she might be expendable—written off as collateral damage. Legate was capable of murder; Roman couldn't take that risk. Better to lay low, keep Anya in the dark.

He circled his bedroom again and came to a halt before his desk. "Computer on."

"Hello, Roman. It's 2:23." In her husky voice, the computer continued. "You have a message from Maureen."

He'd programmed his computer to give him direct warning on several e-mails, including Maureen. "Computer, access the message."

In seconds, the screen displayed an e-mail. "Please call me soon. I miss you."

That was their code. She needed to contact him.

"Computer, secure phone line."

He routinely swept his house for bugs, and in his bedroom he had installed sophisticated antisurveillance technology, including a secure landline telephone. This was, possibly, the only place on earth where he could trust he had privacy.

He punched in Maureen's number. The phone rang half a dozen times before she picked up.

"Hi, Roman."

"What's up?"

"Not me. Sane people are in bed at this hour. Why didn't you call earlier?"

"I just got your message." He made no apology; their contacts never followed a regular nine-to-five pattern. "Why did you call me?"

"First thing." She hesitated, and he heard rustling as if she was getting out of bed. "We don't have enough man power to assign another agent. So you're stuck with me."

"Always a pleasure."

"Second thing. I have information on your former assistant who disappeared. Peter Bunch. He's safe."

Roman was glad to hear that nothing unfortunate had happened to his bright, young assistant. But he wanted to know more. Was Peter Bunch involved with the CIA? "I thought you might know Bunch. Were you dating him, too?"

"He's not one of ours," she said. "He's connected with SCAT, Wade Bouchard's organization."

Oh, swell. All he needed was Anya's father getting involved with his already complicated undercover investigation. "Tell me more about SCAT."

"Noble goals. Questionable methods of achieving them. They're like Greenpeace or PETA—"

"Or the CIA," he said.

"Interesting comparison. The difference is that the CIA operates within the law." She paused. "We have reason to believe Legate is the current target of SCAT's investigations."

"Why?"

"Some of their top guys are in the area. Not that we've had a chance to talk to them. They're like ghosts. Every time we find them, they vanish."

Not surprising. The people involved with Wade Bouchard were brilliant scientists, physicists and humanists. They had the type of minds that would relish the challenge of eluding the CIA. Roman repeated, "Why are they focused on Legate?"

"The Topaku epidemic. Do you remember that project?"

How could he forget that tragedy? A year ago, the small village of Topaku in central Africa had been wiped out by a viral infection that matched a strain that had been isolated by a laboratory in Paris. Legate was hired by the Paris lab to advise on Biosafety Level 4 containment procedures and to create an antiviral vaccine.

When the epidemic occurred in Topaku, Legate was quick to respond. Though they were unable to save the village, they successfully prevented the spread of disease. It was one time when Roman was proud to be working for Legate. "What about Topaku?"

"SCAT suspects wrongdoing."

"They're idiots," Roman said. "In Topaku, Legate behaved brilliantly. If our containment people hadn't acted so quickly, the virus might have wiped out thousands."

Maureen exhaled a sigh. "You know, it's after two in the morning. I don't need a lecture."

Roman himself had worked on the mobilization for Topaku. "Within twenty-four hours, we were—"

"I know," she snapped. "Do you want to hear what I have to say or not?"

"Go ahead."

"SCAT believes there's a piece of evidence in the Legate archives, relating to the Topaku epidemic and damaging to Legate's handling of the situation. The problem is that it's written in an obscure African language. You can't just go in and find it."

"Then why did you call me?"

Maureen cleared her throat. "Is it possible for you to get Anya to translate?"

"Not a chance." No way would he directly involve Anya in this investigation.

"Consider it, Roman."

"No," he said more firmly. "I still don't believe Legate did anything wrong. What do you suspect?"

"We're talking about an Ebola-like virus that could be used in bioterrorism. Not to mention that Legate engineered an expedited penetration into Africa where weapons might have been shipped along with medical supplies. Offhand, I can think of several ways Legate might have capitalized on the situation.'' Her voice was impatient. ''If we find evidence, the CIA can move against Legate. Slater will be out of business.''

Of course, that was his end goal. Disarming Slater and Legate. But Roman had another agenda: Jeremy's death. He wanted to know why his friend had been murdered.

When the reign of Legate was ended, he wanted it to happen for the right reason: because they'd killed their own scientists. They'd taken his friend's life and left Anya a widow.

Into the phone, he said, ''I'll see what I can do to find this memo.''

''Stay in touch,'' Maureen said.

Roman hung up the phone and went downstairs to the sliding glass doors. Stepping onto his deck, the night chill descended from swirling stars and wrapped around him. Icy fingers stroked his naked flesh. The thick redwood planks were rough against his bare feet as he walked to the railing and stood in the very spot where he'd kissed Anya.

Leaning against the railing, he looked down into the splashing waves and luminescent froth of the bay. He wanted revenge for the death of her husband. For her pain.

But there was more at stake. God help him, he wanted Anya for himself.

ON MONDAY MORNING, Roman caught up with Anya on the pathway leading to the Legate mansion. Though he'd spoken to her twice on the phone over the weekend, their conversations had been abrupt. ''Wait up, Anya.''

She stepped off the pathway and stood, sheltered beneath the tangled branches of a Monterey cypress. In her sweater and jeans with a book bag slung over her shoulder, she looked like a student.

She greeted him with a warm smile. "I'm on my way to work."

"That's exactly what I wanted to talk to you about." Together, they strolled at a leisurely pace, and he savored this autumn moment. "I want to get you started on some more complicated translations."

"Which are?"

"In the archives."

Though he'd decided to search for the memo, he wouldn't involve Anya—except as his cover story for digging around in the archives. If questioned about his sudden interest in old documents, Roman would inform Slater that he was simply trying to find more challenging work for Charlie's mother—something to keep her busy. Still, he asked, "How are you with African languages?"

"I know a little Swahili."

"Anything else?"

"You have to be more specific, Roman. There are something like six hundred different dialects in Africa. Many are based on Swahili or Bantu, but they're all unique."

"Suppose I handed you a document in one of these fringe dialects. Could you work out a translation?"

"I could try," she said.

They entered the mansion through the rear door and passed the dining area where a gourmet buffet brunch was arrayed on linen tablecloths.

Roman checked in at the front reception desk. After Anya and Jane Coopersmith exchanged friendly greetings, he teased the receptionist, "Did you miss me, Jane?"

She pushed her thick glasses up on her nose and said, "No messages."

"Not even one? Nobody wants me?"

"Define 'want,'" Jane said, deadpan.

He shrugged and turned toward Anya. "Apparently no-body wants me. No yearning, no lusting, no aching desire."

"Apparently not," she said.

To Jane, he said, "I'll be down in the archives with Anya.

Behind her glasses, Jane's eyebrows lowered in a scowl. Visits to the archives were unusual, and Roman knew that she would store that byte of information in her computer-like brain. Not that it was necessary for Jane to betray his whereabouts. Surveillance was everywhere.

At the rear of the center entry hall, he escorted Anya to a humble-looking wooden door beneath the sweeping stair-case. He placed his thumb on a keypad, got a green light and opened the entrance to a staircase leading down. "When the mansion was originally built, the basement was used for storage. There's still a wine cellar and a couple of temperature-controlled rooms where artwork is stored."

"More paintings? It already seems like every square inch of wall space is covered with art."

"The Legate collection is huge," he said. "We do a lot of international consultation, and grateful clients sometimes show their appreciation with special gifts."

"Any hidden masterpieces?"

"Nothing hidden." One of the first places Roman looked when he began to suspect Legate of wrongdoing was the art collection. Each piece was appraised annually and ac-counted for. Art was a by-product for Fredrick Slater. His only real love was power.

As they proceeded down a narrow corridor, Roman said, "Most of the basement has been converted to archives. A lot of publications and a gazillion reams of paper."

"Isn't all this information on computer?" she asked.

"Of course," he said. "But we need to keep original

contracts with signatures for legal reasons. And we hold on to a lot of the original scientific paperwork because—"

"I know why," she said. "The margin notes are sometimes more important than what's finally published. Jeremy always worked out his formulas on paper."

"I bugged him about that habit."

On the day of the explosion, Roman remembered how Jeremy had been jotting down notes and coughing, eschewing the use of his laptop. The memory was vivid, and Roman guiltily erased it from his mind. He didn't think his old friend would approve of getting Anya involved in this investigation…even indirectly.

"What are we looking for down here?" Anya asked.

"A comparative study. I want you to check the various translations against each other, giving a complete version of research and conclusion."

"Are you sure we can't do this on computer?"

"Not with the margin notes."

Consulting a computer wouldn't work for his true purposes. He doubted that Slater would trust a computer for storing a potentially damaging document, even if it was written in Bantu. Plus, there was no way for him to search for such information without leaving cyberfingerprints. The print archives provided a less traceable source.

He came to a stop outside a double door, went through the thumbprint procedure and opened it. In the archives, the surveillance was blatant. Omnipresent cameras recorded every step they took.

"It's not musty at all," she said. "I would have thought a basement would be damp."

"Temperature and humidity controlled," he said. "We don't want all this paper to rot."

He gestured toward floor-to-ceiling rows of shelves, stacked with cardboard crates and packed with books and bound journals. The sheer volume of material was daunting, but Roman assumed he was dealing with information from the past year—from the time the Paris laboratory consulted Legate.

"Tell me what needs translating," she said.

He didn't want to go directly to the most likely files, not while cameras were watching. First, he needed to establish his cover—finding unsuspicious documents for Anya to work on. "I think there were studies on in vitro fertilization."

"I'd love to look into that," she said enthusiastically. "Where do we start? Under *F* for fertility? Or *B* for baby?"

"I'm not sure." He stepped between the towering aisles and scanned the labels on sturdy packing boxes. For someone like him—accustomed to a talking computer—this search was like returning to the Dark Ages. "How did people find things before computers?"

"Digging," she said. "I love this stuff. I was always a library rat."

He stepped back. "Go for it."

Slowly, she meandered, squinting up at the labels with intent concentration. Her eyes widened when she spied a promising container. Then she shook her head and moved on.

Roman could have stood there all day, watching her. "It's quiet down here."

"Nothing but a hum from the air conditioner."

"We're alone." Except for the cameras, the constant eyes of Legate that pried into every corner of his life. At the end of an aisle, he leaned against the concrete wall, forcing himself not to glare angrily at the camera's lens. "Anya, I want to talk to you about—"

"I know," she said.

How could she? He wasn't even sure himself what he intended to say. "What?"

"You want to talk about this."

She placed her hands on his chest and went up on tiptoe to kiss him. Her lips were tentative as the flutter of a butterfly's wing. Barely touching him, she felt ephemeral as though she was a dream version of Anya, insubstantial and unreal.

To reassure himself that this unexpected moment wasn't a fantasy, his arms encircled her slender body and pulled her close, molding her tightly to him.

He kissed her harder. His tongue penetrated her mouth, gliding through her teeth.

The cameras were watching. Their actions were being recorded. He should stop. He should be a gentleman. But passion overwhelmed reason. Their kiss was lengthy, delectable and thorough.

Breathing rapidly, she leaned away from him. "You weren't kidding about aching desire."

"Only for you."

"Liar."

Though her accusation was spoken in a light, teasing tone, her accuracy stunned him. He was lying to her about a lot of things. His undercover investigation. Her husband's death. The real reason for being here in the archives. "I'm sorry, Anya. I shouldn't have done that."

"But I kissed you," she said.

With all his heart, he wished they were really alone. He whispered in her ear, "I don't want to do anything to hurt you."

"I'm a big girl, Roman. I take responsibility for myself." She disengaged herself from his grasp. "I thought about our kiss all weekend."

"So did I," he said.

"And I decided that I'm ready—absolutely ready—to have some fun."

"What does that mean?"

"At your house, when you kissed me, I felt so alive. And I wanted more."

Peeking up through her lashes, her gaze was shy. But her words were unnervingly direct. "So did I," he said.

"I've never believed in beating around the bush," she said. The quiver in her voice betrayed her inner turmoil, but she continued determinedly. "The way I figure, you're the safest man in the world for a fling because you're a confirmed bachelor. We won't have to worry about sticky emotional involvements."

Roman couldn't believe what he was hearing. This was his speech—the one he gave to women who had marriage in mind. Roman was always careful to tell them that they were only here for the moment, enjoying themselves, seizing the day.

Anya continued. "You understand, don't you? We can…experiment like this. And it doesn't mean anything."

"A kiss is just a kiss," he said.

"Right." She reached up to tidy her hair. The angle of her arm and the arch of her throat fascinated him. She was so delicate and fine. "Now, let's find those documents you want me to review."

He watched as she browsed through the shelves. Fortunately, this trip to the archives was merely a ruse to set up other visits because his powers of concentration were completely wiped out. All he could think about was Anya—her body, her beauty and her determined quest for fun.

IN THE LATE AFTERNOON, Fredrick Slater stood at the arched window of his office, surveying the grounds. He saw his chief administrator, Roman Alexander, walking with

Anya. As was his habit, Slater matched them genetically. Both tall. Both attractive and fit. Their combined DNA would create an excellent physical specimen if they reproduced. But not a genius like Charlie.

The thought of the boy pleased him. Young Charlie was an intellectual sponge—able to grasp difficult concepts with minimal exertion. A magnificent future lay before him. He would lead Legate.

But Charlie's mother was a problem. Slater thought he'd disarmed Anya by suggesting to Roman that he become involved with her. He expected the young woman to be distracted by love, allowing him to wean Charlie from her. But Anya was a mother first. Utterly devoted to her child.

And Roman had been behaving suspiciously of late. Neville often warned that Roman was a potential threat who should be under constant surveillance. Risk-aggressive and headstrong, Roman might take matters into his own hands if he suspected wrongdoing.

Earlier today, he'd mentioned African dialects to Anya. Why? What was he looking for?

Slater crossed the room and went to one of three wall safes. This one was hidden behind a small Degas, and it was refrigerated. In here, he kept top secret specimens. Three vials were labeled Topaku.

Chapter Six

The day before Halloween, Anya was almost ready to leave her cottage when she heard a knock on the door. Had Roman come here? She thought they'd agreed to meet in the parking lot. "Just a sec," she called out.

For the past several days, the fun part of their relationship proceeded at an unexpectedly restrained pace, one baby step at a time. After her announcement to Roman in the archives, she had expected a more outright sexual approach.

Instead, Roman seemed to be courting her. He spent time with her, talking and sharing lunch in the opulent employee dining room. They reviewed her archive projects and joined Charlie at the stables for a horseback ride.

But there hadn't been as much kissing as she wanted. Being with Roman was like swallowing hot chili peppers that started with a tingle in your throat, then exploded in your mouth. A fire was building inside her, and she hoped Roman would hurry up and quench the flame.

There was another knock on the door.

"Hang on," she said. "I'm almost there."

She checked her reflection in the mirror. Her forest-green turtleneck and jeans were the perfect outfit for an afternoon of shopping for Halloween supplies. But she was hoping this expedition might evolve into something more sensual. Quickly, she changed into a clingy red sweater with a low-cut neckline. The red ought to be a signal, like waving a matador's cape in front of a bull. *Get the hint, Roman. I'm ready.*

She fluttered her eyelashes at her reflection in the mirror and arranged her mouth in a come-hither smile. As soon as she opened the door, her grin vanished. "Mother?"

"It took you long enough to answer."

Claudette swept inside and scanned the cottage with a steady, efficient gaze before she picked up the green turtle-neck that Anya had tossed over a chairback. "You still haven't done much with this place."

"It doesn't need much." Anya's belongings had arrived from Denver. She'd replaced some of the pictures on the walls and filled the shelves with her own books and knick-knacks. "I prefer the furniture that was already here."

Claudette folded the turtleneck and placed it on a table near the staircase. "You could have saved a lot of trouble and expense if you'd decided that before I went to Denver to supervise the movers. Why bother with transporting all your old stuff out here and putting it in storage?"

Because she might someday change her mind about living here. Because she still couldn't bear to sort through all the things she'd bought with Jeremy and decide which were precious and which were junk. Anya knew it was useless to explain emotional reasons to her mother. Though Claudette was a brilliant medical consultant, there were some things she simply couldn't comprehend. "What brings you to Legate?"

"A lunch date with Fredrick." She patted her tidy French twist, and her thin lips pursed in a smug grin. "He's a very attractive man, you know."

Ugh! Don't go there. Though Fredrick Slater was, in a

way, Anya's benefactor, she didn't particularly like the man. "Glad you're enjoying his company, Mother."

"Besides, I don't need an invitation to visit my only daughter, do I?" She reached into the pocket of her trench coat and held up a pamphlet. "Jane Coopersmith asked me to drop off this information you requested."

"Thanks." Anya accepted the brochure for an international language school with classes in San Francisco.

"Planning to take some refresher courses?"

"I need more training in African and Serbian dialects," Anya said. "I'm out of my depth in translating some of these obscure documents."

"That language school is in San Francisco, and all the classes are at night." Obviously, Claudette had read the brochure. So much for privacy. "How will you manage that? You can't leave Charlie here alone."

"I'll find a baby-sitter."

She exhaled a long-suffering sigh. "I can take care of him."

"Not necessary."

"I'll do it," she said firmly. "You and I can trade places for the night. You'll stay at my house in the city, and I'll spend the night here."

The last thing Anya wanted was her mother taking up residence in the guest bedroom. "Really, Mother. I couldn't ask—"

"Nonsense! I need to spend some alone time with my grandson. It'll be *fun*." She emphasized the last word. "You're always saying you want more *fun*."

Defensively, Anya changed the subject. "Are you ready for Halloween?"

"I haven't quite decided on my costume. A few years ago, I bought a little French maid outfit. It's probably not appropriate for the children."

"Probably not."

"But I still have the legs for it." She pushed aside her trench coat and admiringly studied her slender calves that tapered down to a size five shoe. "Fredrick would like me as a saucy French maid."

Double ugh! Anya held up her hand. "Too much information, Mother."

"You have no room to talk, dear. From what I've heard, you and Roman are quite the hot item."

No way was Anya going to discuss her relationship with Claudette. "As a matter of fact, I was just heading out to meet Roman. We're going to do some Halloween shopping."

"Shopping?" Claudette's tone was suggestive. "Is that what they're calling sex these days?"

Anya ignored the innuendo. "I'm meeting him in front of the mansion, so I can walk back there with you."

"I'll stay here," Claudette announced as she took off her coat. "That way you won't have to rush home to take care of Charlie."

Charlie wasn't out of school for another three hours, and Anya expected to be home by then. But she didn't argue with her mother. Years of experience had taught her that once Claudette made up her mind, there was no changing it. "Fine. I'll be back in a couple of hours."

Her plan had been to bring Roman back here to the cottage. After dinner and putting Charlie to bed, she thought they might…shop, if that's what they were calling it these days.

"Anya," her mother snapped.

"Yes, Mother."

"Be careful, dear."

It was an odd thing to say, but this surprise visit from Claudette had been very weird. A French maid's outfit? Sex with Fredrick Slater? Anya shuddered as she slipped into her black pea coat, went outside and hurried along the pathway.

The earthy smell of autumn hung in the air, and the skies were that ominous shade of gray that came before a storm. Why had her mother warned her to be careful?

At the parking lot, Anya spied Roman standing beside his Mercedes, talking on his cell phone. She rushed up to him. "Am I late?"

He ended the call. "You're worth the wait."

So was he. Dressed for work in a pin-striped suit under a long, cashmere camel coat, Roman looked as if he might have stepped from the pages of *GQ*. Seeing him made her feel immeasurably better.

When he turned toward his Mercedes, she said, "Wait. Let's take my minivan."

He gave a deprecating snort—the typical bachelor's reaction to a family-oriented vehicle. "Why?"

"We're shopping for Halloween supplies, and they take up a lot of space. I might want to buy a huge skeleton or something."

"Okay," he muttered. "But I'm driving."

She tossed him the car keys and headed across the parking lot toward her respectable blue Caravan. As she climbed into the passenger seat, she patted the dashboard and whispered a reassurance, "It's okay, Vanna. I think you're beautiful."

He adjusted the driver's seat to suit his long legs. "I can't believe you have a name for this donkey."

"Hey, if you can have a female computer, I can name my car which is, by the way, a useful size for packing in kids and supplies."

"Not to mention the main safety feature," he muttered. "You can't go fast enough to get into serious trouble."

Before she fastened her seat belt, she considered taking off her jacket to give him a glimpse of the sexy red sweater, then decided against it. The man had insulted her car; he didn't deserve a cleavage view.

"Where to?" he asked.

"Some kind of mall. I want to get trick-or-treat candy and fake spiderwebs and maybe a rubber snake or two. I've already got a wind-up Frankenstein that says, 'Fire! Bad!'"

"You're a crazy lady." He grinned as he navigated through the Legate parking lot. "Of course, I mean that in the best possible way."

"Speaking of crazy, I can't believe how Legate gets into this Halloween costume thing. I heard that the geneticists plan to link themselves together in a DNA strand. And a bunch of people are dressing up like mad scientists."

"Which isn't really much of a stretch."

Roman turned north on Central Avenue. Though South Shore Shopping Center was closer, he needed to go into Oakland to pick up the finishing touch for his own costume.

As he adjusted the rearview mirror, he noticed a black sedan with tinted windows. He'd seen that car before.

"My mother stopped by," Anya said. "She's dating Fredrick Slater."

"Doesn't surprise me." Claudette and Slater were two of a kind—ruthless, ambitious and smart. "They have a lot in common."

"Mother is taking a real interest in Charlie." When she mentioned her son's name, Anya smiled. "Moving here was the right thing for him. He's happy at this school. There's enough stimulating information to keep him interested. And he still has time for play."

Half listening, Roman kept an eye on the black sedan in the rearview mirror. He couldn't tell if the other car was tailing the minivan. This was the main road leading to Oakland, and it was logical for anybody who lived in the area to take it.

He decided to pull over and let the other car pass.

As he eased onto the shoulder, Anya asked, "What are you doing?"

"I thought I heard a clunking noise in the engine."

She leaned forward, listening. "I had some work done on the transmission last year. I hope there's nothing else wrong."

He pretended to listen as he watched the sedan cruise past them. It was impossible to see the passengers through the tinted windows, and he caught only a fleeting glimpse of the license plate. The car was an Intrepid with a couple of years on it.

"I don't hear anything," she said.

"Me, neither. Guess I was wrong." He merged back onto the road. "Any other news from Claudette?"

"She volunteered to baby-sit while I take a class at the Institute of International Languages. I'll be gone one night a week."

"Going into the city?"

"I'm looking forward to it," she said. "It's a shame to live so close and never get into town."

But he didn't like the idea of Anya wandering around San Francisco alone and unguarded. Legate had enemies. Worse than that, *Legate was the enemy.*

Until he put together the last pieces of the puzzle, he wanted Anya to be where he could keep an eye on her, especially now that he'd slipped her a few unimportant memos on the Topaku epidemic so he could dig deeper into the files.

Thus far, he'd found nothing to indicate Legate acted inappropriately. Maureen must have been mistaken about the possible evidence from the archives.

He turned back to Anya. "What languages are you taking?"

"I'm thinking of Serbian and African dialects," she said. "I'm fascinated by the work of a Polish doctor on in vitro fertilization."

"Because of your own experience?"

She nodded. "I never thought I'd get pregnant. When Jeremy found out about the Legate experiments, I was looking into adoption."

"Would you have been happy with an adoption?"

"Absolutely," she said. "It was Jeremy who was determined to make a baby. Maybe because it was his fault that…" Her voice trailed off.

"I know," Roman said. Jeremy blamed himself for the couple's infertility. From working in biochemistry labs, he came in contact with many toxins, bacteria and viruses. He believed that he contracted a low-grade infection that affected his sperm count. "It all worked out for the best."

"Charlie?" She beamed. "He's the best. That's for sure."

As they crossed the bridge, Roman spotted the black Intrepid, parked at a turnoff. It pulled into traffic behind them. If this was surveillance, it was damn clumsy—almost as if they wanted him to notice.

If he'd been alone, he would have forced a showdown with whoever was driving that car. But he wouldn't put Anya in danger. The only alternative was to lose the car that was tailing them.

"This Polish fertility doctor," Anya said, "makes reference to a paper by Dr. Neville on bonding. But I didn't see anything from him in the files."

"Possibly he keeps that information in his personal papers."

"I ought to ask him."

Her statement registered in his mind. He didn't want Anya talking to Neville—nothing good could come from that contact.

Right now, Roman focused on the sedan in his rearview mirror. He needed to get off the main streets where the traffic was too tight to maneuver. With a glance over his shoulder, he swooped across two lanes to make a sudden sharp left.

"Hey," Anya said, "what are you doing?"

"This is a shortcut. It'll give Vanna a chance to show her stuff."

"Her stuff?" she questioned. "Her stuff is reliability and a decent ride and—"

"What kind of engine have you got?"

"Four perky little cylinders."

"Terrific." They might be able to outrun a moped, but a high-speed chase was out of the question. Nor could he count on great maneuverability. This was like driving a shoe box.

As he made another sharp left, Vanna tilted precariously. The tires squealed.

"Roman! Stop it!"

The black car was still on their tail, and they didn't care if he knew it. What were they after?

He tromped on the gas pedal, and the minivan lurched forward in a pathetic surge. Almost immediately, he tapped the brake. They were in a residential area where cars parked haphazardly and kids chased soccer balls into the street. He couldn't speed through here.

He tried to visualize what would happen if he slammed on the brake and attempted a quick turnaround. The minivan would probably stop dead in its tracks. Then what? Roman wasn't armed. He had no way of dealing with an attacker.

Another quick turn.

In the rearview mirror, he saw the black sedan keep going straight. They were no longer following. Roman circled a few more blocks. There was no sign of the other vehicle.

"Sorry," he said to Anya. "I got turned around."

"What's going on?" Her voice was serious.

"Just trying to save a couple minutes."

"I don't believe you," she said. "You were driving like you were trying to escape. Was someone following us?"

"Why would anyone be tailing us?"

He hated lying to her, but there was no way to explain that Legate was evil and he was working with the CIA. He couldn't blow his cover. Not even with her.

"Roman, tell me the truth."

He shrugged. "I have a rotten sense of direction."

"You want me to believe that all this wheeling around and bad driving is because you got lost?"

"Yes," he said. "I want you to believe that."

He felt her gaze boring into his skull and reading his mind. She was much too smart for Roman to keep her in blissful ignorance.

Back on the main road again, he searched frantically for a diversion. "Look over there. A giant drugstore." He exited into the parking lot. "They ought to have all the rubber snakes you need."

"You're not going to tell me what's really going on, are you?"

He pulled into a vacant space. "Halloween is tomorrow, and you need to shop."

Outside the minivan, he surveyed the parking lot. Though he didn't see the black sedan, there were a lot of cars, which also meant there were plenty of witnesses. Nobody would come after them here.

Still watching for threats, Roman escorted her toward a

doorway where a banner proclaimed that this store was Halloween Headquarters. As they stepped onto the curb, the black Intrepid pulled up. Acting on instinct, Roman stepped in front of Anya, shielding her.

Peter Bunch emerged from the passenger side. "Hey, Roman. I thought I recognized you."

His former assistant looked pretty damn healthy for a supposedly missing person who was now working for SCAT. "Hello, Peter."

"Can we talk? I wanted to ask you about something."

"Sure." He turned to Anya. "Go inside and get started. I'll join you."

Her blue eyes flared with anger. Then, without a word, she turned on her heel and went into the store.

"She's a pretty lady," Peter said.

"What the hell is that supposed to mean?"

"I'm just making an observation."

Roman took a step toward the Intrepid, and it pulled away. He memorized the license plate before turning back toward Peter, the shaggy-haired, young man who should have had a bright future. "Why were you following me?"

"Hey, I'm with the good guys."

"SCAT," Roman said. He didn't trust Anya's father and his crackpot gang of wayward scientists. "You're with SCAT."

"Maybe." Peter looked down at the toe of his worn sneakers, sheepish as a third-grader whose dog ate his homework. "I want to warn you about some stuff going on at Legate. People are starting to suspect you."

"What people?" Roman snapped. "Give me specifics, Peter."

"I shouldn't even be talking to you." He bit his lower

lip, but he didn't seem afraid. There was an impudence about him and a hint of fanaticism. But what was his cause?

"If you have something to say, go ahead."

When Peter looked up, his boyish manner was gone. His eyes were hard, cold and calculating. "It's about Charlie."

Chapter Seven

Stalking the aisles of the brightly lit superstore, Anya rattled her shopping cart. She was plenty ticked off. Not only did Roman shove her out of the way when that strange young man confronted them, but he lied to her face. A shortcut, my eye! She knew someone had been following them. Did he think she was incapable of handling that information? Was he trying to protect her? From what?

When she turned, she spied Roman coming toward her…and she wasn't the only one who noticed him. A couple of other women giggled. Another stared. In his cashmere coat with his necktie loosened and his black hair mussed by the wind, he was much too classy and gorgeous to be hanging out in the Halloween aisle.

Anya took a closer look at him. Tension pulled at the corners of his mouth, and the faint lines at the corners of his eyes tightened. He looked like a man with a deep, dark secret. And she meant to find out what it was.

He pointed at her empty shopping cart. "Can't make up your mind?"

"Who was that man?"

"A former associate." He picked up a bag of chocolate kisses. "How about this?"

"I'm getting full-size candy bars," she said. There was

enough money in her savings account to splurge. "Why didn't you introduce me to this former associate?"

"He left Legate in bad standing. It's better if you don't know him."

"What are you hiding from me?"

The muscles in his jaw twitched and then relaxed. In two blinks, the obvious signs of edginess vanished. His shoulders straightened, and his outer appearance became the very definition of suave. "Let's forget about that guy, shall we? You and I should concentrate on what's really important. Halloween."

His voice cajoled her, and she remembered that Roman was a master negotiator. That was his job.

Doggedly, she said, "I want to know the truth."

With an easy grin, he guided her away from the candy display where other Halloween shoppers were reaching around them. In a deserted aisle that blossomed with fake greenery, he selected a red silk rose and presented it to her. "Forgive me, Anya. I've behaved badly today."

She twirled the rose between her fingers. He was smooth as silk, cleverly diverting her attention. "That was a very pretty apology."

"Accepted?"

"Not until you tell me what's going on." Behind his deep-set eyes and high cheekbones, she saw a brick wall. But her stubbornness was a match for his. "The truth, Roman."

"For right now you'll have to trust me."

"How can I trust you when you're obviously hiding something?"

"Because I asked you to," he said.

"That's not enough." Damn it! Less than an hour ago, she'd been strategizing on how to get him into bed. Not anymore! She wouldn't tumble for a man she couldn't trust.

"Okay." He rubbed his hands together as if everything had been settled. He had nothing further to say. "Let's get this shopping done."

When Roman turned and walked back toward the Halloween display, he felt a tug on his heart as if a piece of it had been torn away. She didn't trust him. And he couldn't blame her.

He was withholding the truth from her. An unfortunate necessity. If he shared all he knew, she'd be in certain danger.

The information Peter Bunch had given him about Charlie was devastating, to say the least. Even after Roman had an opportunity to verify Peter's allegations, he wasn't sure that he'd tell Anya the truth about her son. Some things were better left unknown.

THE WEATHER on Halloween morning dawned bright and clear, but Anya had an angry little storm cloud hovering above her head. Yesterday, the possibility of a hot, sexy liaison with Roman had been shattered.

Today had to be better. She put the finishing touches on her costume. Since Charlie was a mummy—wrapped from head to toe in miles of torn-up sheets—she decided to be Nefertiti. She wore a white caftan cinched at the waist with gold braid. A black and gold headdress covered her white-blond hair, and her eye makeup was painted on with a trowel.

Charlie applauded as she walked into the kitchen. "You look pretty, Mommy."

"I'm not the mummy," she teased. "You're the mummy."

He adjusted the sheet bandages that she'd stitched to his pants and shirt so his costume wouldn't end up in a puddle around his feet. He glowered under his mummy cap of drooping bandages. "Do I look scary?"

He looked adorable. "Terrifying."

"I should put some catsup on me. Like blood."

"But if you're really a mummy," she said, "you wouldn't bleed."

He hunched his shoulders and raised his hands like claws. Then he growled. "The blood comes from my victims."

She grinned. So much for being unscary. Her son couldn't wait to terrorize the other kids. Last night, when they'd decorated the cottage, he'd focused on the dangling spiderwebs and skeletons, leaving the happy pumpkin cutouts in the bag.

He finished his cereal and jumped down from his chair. "I'm going to school now."

"Let me grab a cup of coffee, and I'll walk you over."

"It's okay." He was already at the door. "You don't have to."

"Wait a minute, mister." Though his walk to school was merely a half-mile hike across the well-patrolled Legate grounds, she didn't want to abandon this morning ritual. She trailed Charlie onto the porch.

"Hey," he yelled. "Come here, Harrison."

The armed guard appeared out of nowhere—a particularly irritating habit that Anya still hadn't gotten used to. Harrison gave her a friendly smile. "Good morning, ma'am. Nice outfit."

"And what are you going to be for Halloween?"

"I thought I might wear a suit and carry a briefcase."

"That's not scary," Charlie said.

"It is to me," Harrison replied.

Charlie hopped down the three steps to the pathway. "Harrison can walk to school with me."

"He probably has other things to do," Anya said.

"Not really, ma'am." He slung his high-powered, automatic rifle over his shoulder. "I can walk with Charlie. No problem-o."

The problem was Anya's. She wanted to walk with her son, to hold his little hand and listen to his morning conversation. She wanted him to need her. But he'd already latched on to Harrison.

"Wait, Charlie." She came down the steps after him. "Give me a hug."

"Mummies don't hug."

"But mommies do." She gathered him into her arms and squeezed. "I love you, sweetpea."

"Bye, Mom."

And he was off without a glance over his shoulder. Walking away from her. Standing on his own.

This was a milestone. Though she was proud of his independent nature, she was also bereft. Her baby was growing up. She watched Charlie until he was out of sight, tears welling up behind her eyelids. She remembered him as an infant, helpless and squalling. His first word. His first step.

Anya choked back sobs. She couldn't start crying. Not with all this Nefertiti makeup.

She grabbed her backpack and set out toward the mansion. Before checking in at her library cubicle, she intended to visit Dr. Neville and ask him if she could have access to his private files on the in vitro experiments and the psychological aftermath in terms of bonding and parenting. The timing for her to read this study might be especially appropriate. Was it harder for someone like Anya—someone who had gone through years of struggling to conceive a child—to let go of her baby? Was the bond stronger or more fragile?

She entered the front foyer and waved to Jane Coopersmith. "Where's your costume, Jane?"

She pushed back her hair to reveal pointy alien ears. Her hand raised in the split-finger Vulcan salute from *Star Trek.* "Live long and prosper."

"Cool," Anya said.

"Spock is one of my heroes."

Very appropriate for a woman who operated with utterly dispassionate, machinelike competence. Anya wished she could have been more friendly with Jane, who was one of the few other employees who lived on the Legate grounds.

Anya hiked up the center staircase to Dr. Neville's office. His door was ajar, and she stepped inside. Neville's assistant was away from her desk, and a tall man in a floor-length black cape leaned over the file cabinets.

Roman turned to face her. He was dressed as Dracula in a black tuxedo with gleaming white shirt under a scarlet-lined cape. His thick black hair was combed straight back from his forehead. He was scary in the sense that she'd never seen a more regal, dashing, handsome man...or vampire.

When he smiled warmly at her, she noticed the important detail his costume lacked. "Fangs?"

"You're welcome."

She stifled a chuckle. How could she stay mad at him? When he turned on the charm, Roman was irresistible. Still, she kept her distance. "What are you doing here? Is Dr. Neville in?"

He held up a file folder. "I was picking up information for you. This is the paper Neville did on in vitro babies and bonding."

She accepted the file from him and slipped it into her backpack. "Thank you."

"Nice costume. Cleopatra?"

"Nefertiti." She didn't want to have a casual conversation with him, pretending that nothing had happened. She didn't want to talk to him at all. This was a man she no longer could trust.

"And what's Charlie's Halloween disguise?"

"A mummy. He thinks he's terrifying, but he's so cute I can hardly stand it."

"The kids from the school are scheduled to do their trick-or-treating at eleven. Are you planning to—"

"I should be going now," she interrupted before she was drawn into more chat. "Bye."

Her exit was quick but not painless. Each step away from him was accompanied by an annoying twinge of regret. Merely being in the same room with him flushed her cheeks and caused her heart to sing. How could she walk away from all that?

ROMAN FOLLOWED HER out the door and stood at the banister watching her flee. *That was a very close call.* If she'd gotten into Neville's office ahead of him, Anya might have stumbled onto the paper trail that told the truth about Charlie. This was a trail he intended to follow, which meant he had to obtain access to confidential files in the clinic—the medical records for Jeremy, Anya and Charlie. If the information Peter Bunch gave him was correct, Roman couldn't ignore it. He needed to make plans to get Anya and Charlie away from here.

And Legate wasn't the only threat. Roman had traced the license plate of the car Peter Bunch had emerged from. The owner of the vehicle was Chou Liu, a member of SCAT and known associate of Anya's father.

Watching from the second-floor landing, Roman saw Anya run directly into Dr. Neville at the foot of the staircase. This might be trouble. Roman swept down toward them with his Dracula cape flying.

Neville wore his usual gray suit with an orange necktie and matching handkerchief—a fact Roman noted as he burst into the psychiatrist's conversation with Anya. "An orange tie. Is that your costume, Neville?"

"Not entirely." The psychiatrist reached into his pocket, produced a red foam ball and stuck it onto his narrow nose above his mustache. "I'm a clown."

A dangerous clown. The type little children ran away from, Roman thought. "What were you two talking about?"

"That's none of your concern," Anya snapped.

Roman didn't like Neville's measured study of Anya. He didn't want the shrink asking questions. What if she told Neville about the meeting with Peter Bunch?

If Anya said too much, his undercover operation would be compromised. He needed to keep her quiet, but couldn't tell her the real reasons why she needed to hold her tongue. He was walking a tightrope, facing a riddle with no good solution. A conundrum.

Neville broke the silence with a glance at Anya, then at Roman. "Lover's quarrel?" he asked.

"What?" Her eyes were huge inside that ridiculous Nefertiti makeup. "Roman is not my lover."

"I rather had the impression you two were dating," he said slyly. "Is Legate's favorite bachelor off his game?"

"What does that mean?" Anya demanded.

"Well, now…" Neville stepped back a pace. "I should ask, 'What does it mean to you?'"

"That Legate is worse than a small town where everybody's bright red nose is into everybody else's business."

"I see." Neville nodded. "And you feel that all these people are watching you."

"I'm not paranoid, Doctor."

"Of course not," Neville said. "Won't you come up to my office? Anya, we ought to talk."

No way would Roman allow her to confide in this clown. He reached into the conversation and stirred up her hostility. "Excuse me, Neville. Why do you think Anya and I are lovers?"

"You're a very popular member of our staff." His red clown nose twitched. "Especially with the ladies."

"You think I seduced her?"

Below his mustache, Neville's mouth pursed. "I think you have a...relationship."

"Stop right there," Anya said. "I don't want to hear anymore."

She turned on her heel and stalked toward the library.

Roman winked at Neville. "I'd better go after her. By the way, I was in your office. Anya was interested in one of your published papers."

"Which one? I should—"

"Later," Roman said as he left the staircase.

In the library, he went to her cubicle. Seated in her chair, she stared down at Dr. Neville's article. "Wish I had a door," she muttered. "I'd slam it in your face."

Aware that their conversation was probably being monitored somewhere in the Legate security system, Roman chose his words carefully. He knew the key to manipulating Anya: Make reference to Charlie. She'd do anything for her son.

How could he do this to her? He was no better than a cheap con man, pulling the strings, making her do as he needed. From this moment forward, Roman had no claim to high-and-mighty values—even if his efforts resulted in bringing Legate to justice. Deceit lowered him to their level.

When she glared up at him, he sank into the liquid blue of her eyes. Even though she was dressed like a cut-rate Egyptian princess, Anya was a seriously beautiful woman. Her soft full lips pursed in a scowl. Her chin lifted, creating a pleasing line from her throat to her cleavage. He longed to caress her face, to gather her body against him, to protect her from all these world-shaking conspiracies.

"Well?" Her tone was hard. "Are you just going to stand there?"

"I'm thinking of what I should say."

"How about 'goodbye'?"

"Pushing me away won't do any good," he said. "This place is too small to avoid each other."

"I can give it a try," she said.

"That's not fair to Charlie." The instant he mentioned her son, her cold gaze flickered. Roman played his ace card. "Your son and I have a relationship whether you like it or not."

"I don't trust you, Roman. Not anymore. Why should I encourage your friendship with Charlie?"

"Because I'm a direct link with his father." He played his trump card. "Jeremy and I grew up together. I can tell stories that Charlie wouldn't otherwise know."

"Not true." Her voice quavered. "I know all about—"

"These are guy things." Roman pressed his advantage even though he knew he was hurting her. "I know the kind of stuff a father and son would share."

She shook her head angrily. "Jeremy and I talked about everything."

"Everything?" Roman questioned. He was about to win this game of wits. A hollow triumph. "Then why didn't your husband tell you that he signed Charlie up for the Legate school?"

A startled gasp escaped her lips.

His instinct was to reach out, to soothe her pain and tell her that he was wrong. Jeremy trusted her. Charlie loved her. She was a terrific mother and wife.

But if he took pity on her now, he would lose his edge. "You need me, Anya."

When she looked up, her gaze was sharp and clear. She seemed focused. "I'll call a truce," she said. "For Charlie's sake."

"One more thing," he said. "You're right about this place being a gossip mill. Anything that happens between us is private."

"Agreed."

He clarified. "No little chats with Neville."

"No way. I hate having people poke into my life." She stared at him with undisguised disgust. The message was clear: She didn't want Roman in her life, either.

She swiveled around in her chair and stared down at the paper on the desktop in front of her, dismissing him.

He left with a swoosh of his Dracula cape. The vampire costume suited him well; he'd sucked the blood from what might have been a decent relationship with Anya.

As he went through his morning routine, he couldn't stop thinking about her. The anger and hurt in her eyes haunted him. There should have been a better way for him to gain her cooperation. He shouldn't have forced her.

At eleven o'clock, when the kids started their trick-or-treating rounds, he joined the Halloween parade from one department to another. Anya was part of the group. Among the other parents, she stood out. She had a presence, a glow that made her the most appealing woman in any gathering—a woman who, unfortunately, despised him.

All for the best, he thought as he put on his most genial facade. He wouldn't be distracted from his investigation by his attraction to her.

He had already obtained part of the information he needed with a visit to the clinic where he asked for a copy of Anya's medical files under the pretext that he was looking for her birth date. Her birthday wasn't until late spring. Not soon enough for him to give her a gift that would make her forgive him. Like what? He couldn't erase her sorrow, couldn't bring Jeremy back to life, couldn't even provide her with the "fun" she wanted.

Roman watched as the children bounced like jumping beans through the usually silent, sterile Legate offices. Their costumes ranged from the predictable fairy princess to a robot.

Most of the adults reacted with pleasure to the friendly incursion of kids. They were a ray of sunshine in this gray, intellectual world. Morale within the compound was at an all-time high. This should have been a good day for Roman.

Slater, dressed as a ringmaster in riding jodhpurs and red jacket, complimented him. So did Neville, grudgingly. They thought he was doing a good job as administrator.

But he'd never felt more contemptible. He'd hurt Anya, planted self-doubt in her mind.

At six o'clock, he should have gone home, but he couldn't leave without seeing her one more time. Somehow he had to gain a measure of redemption.

He strode along the path toward her cottage, not completely sure what he would say. At the very least, he meant to patch over any crack in her self-esteem.

At her doorstep, he slipped in his Dracula teeth and knocked.

She opened immediately. Though she still wore her costume dress, her face was washed clean of makeup and her long blond hair was free from the ancient Egyptian headdress.

Her gaze was expectant, as though she'd been waiting for something important. Without a word, she flung herself into his arms.

Chapter Eight

The polished white front of his tuxedo shirt glided smoothly against her cheek. Anya clung to him, needing his strength and reassurance. The warmth of his embrace penetrated her skin and started her blood flowing through shriveled empty veins.

"Charlie isn't here," she whispered.

Her son didn't need her anymore; that was her lesson for the day. This morning, he'd walked to school with Harrison. Tonight, Charlie had chosen to go with her mother and Fredrick Slater into San Francisco to watch the Halloween festivities. It was a Friday night. No need for him to rush back for school in the morning. And they had made it perfectly clear—all three of them—that she ought to stay here, supposedly to rest, supposedly to enjoy her time alone.

But she hated her life without Charlie. Being alone at the cottage was deathly quiet.

Tonight, she needed the warmth and solace of another human being. And so she embraced Roman—even though she was angry at him, even though she couldn't trust him. She wanted to make love; she desperately needed the mindless escape of pure animal passion.

Leaning away from his chest, she tipped back her head, eyes closed. "Kiss me," she demanded.

She felt him coming closer. She heard the heated murmur of his breath. His lips brushed her cheeks, her chin. He nuzzled her throat. Something scratched like fingernails.

Her eyelids opened. "What are you doing?"

When his lips parted, she saw his Dracula fangs. "I vant to bite your neck," he said.

Irritated, she shoved at his gleaming shirtfront. How had he stayed so perfectly clean after a full day of work? "This is no time for jokes. I want to have sex with you."

"Needless to say, I'm delighted." He took out his fake teeth. "Mind if I ask why?"

"Because I need someone to be utterly devoted to me and my personal pleasure tonight."

"And I happened to be the lucky guy who came to the door?"

"You're supposedly quite proficient."

"But I'm not a performing seal."

"What do you want, Roman? Foreplay?" She wasn't in the mood for seductive little games. All she wanted from him was sex—hard and fast and messy. She wanted screams of passion to drown out the whimpering sadness in her soul.

"Anya, what's wrong?"

"I don't want to talk." She approached him again. Angrily, she reached up and plucked at his bow tie, unfastening the knot. "How about this for starters? I'll rip your clothes off."

Her fingers trembled as she fumbled with his pearl buttons. She pulled the dress shirt open. Above his T-shirt, his chest was warm, muscular and nicely furry.

He caught hold of her hands. "What the hell is going on?"

She tried to yank away from him, but he held tightly. "Listen, Roman, if you can't handle my needs, I'll open the door and call for Harrison the security guard. He won't ask questions."

"No need." His voice was hard as a slap. "I can handle you."

"Do it," she demanded.

He whirled her around and pinned her against the closed door. "You want it here? Up against the door?"

"Yes, damn you. Right here."

His mouth consumed hers with ferocious intensity. His tongue plunged so deeply into her mouth that she couldn't breathe. His large, muscular body pressed against her. When she tried to put a space between them, he leaned harder. His thigh wedged between her legs, forcing them apart.

She had never been kissed with such overwhelming brute force. He was taking her, plundering her senses. He was a beast—a true vampire.

Just as suddenly, he stepped back. His eyes gleamed with a dangerous, dark, demonic fire. "Is this really what you want?"

Part of her screamed, *Yes, yes, yes!* She dangled at the edge of an abyss, clinging by her fingertips to the edge of reality.

"Tell me now," Roman demanded. "Is this what you want?"

Breathless, she gazed at the intense romantic figure that stood before her. A man who could take her to the brink of passion. Was this what she wanted? Passion without trust?

"No," she said.

He turned away from her and strode toward the kitchen.

Gasping, she leaned her back against the door and closed her eyes. Her heart crashed madly inside her rib cage. Shivers raced across the surface of her skin, but her moment of insane, reckless need had begun to ebb.

What had she been thinking? She was off balance, out of her head. Having mindless sex with Roman was a mistake she might regret for the rest of her life. He'd said cruel things to her today, implied that she needed a man to bring up her son properly, hinted that her relationship with Jeremy hadn't been ideal. Of course, it hadn't been perfect. No husband and wife could claim that every single aspect of their joined life was without flaw.

She pushed herself away from the door. Her knees were weak as she stumbled toward the kitchen where Roman had opened a bottle of wine. "Why did you come here tonight?" she asked.

"I wanted to see you," he said. "The way we left things earlier today…it wasn't right. I shouldn't have said those things to you."

She noticed that he stopped just short of an apology, but she wouldn't hold it against him. Her own behavior hadn't been appropriate; she'd practically mauled him.

"We've both been rude," she said. "Let's call it even."

"Does this mean you're willing to—"

"Be friends again," she said. The sexual part of their relationship was more overwhelming than she could handle at the moment.

"Fair enough."

He handed her a glass of white wine and stepped past her without touching. In the center of her living room, he glanced around and she followed his gaze, taking inventory of her Halloween decorations. Fake cobwebs, festooned with giant tarantulas, draped in the corners. Several jack-o'-lanterns flickered with waning candles—the only light in the room. A headless dummy slouched in the rocking chair.

"Spooky," Roman said.

She struggled to match his calm, cool attitude. "I might as well clean up the decorations. I assume there won't be trick-or-treaters tonight. It's a little hard to get past the armed guards. And Charlie isn't home."

"Where is he?"

"Slater and my mother invited him into town to check out San Francisco's Halloween celebrations. He wanted to go to a haunted house."

"Your mother's place?"

"Claudette can be pretty darn scary."

She took a measured sip of the crisp, dry wine. Her heartbeat was still rapid, but her sense of equilibrium had returned, and she realized how very exhausted she was.

Anya went to one of the ceramic pumpkins and leaned down to blow out the candle. The ambient light in the room dimmed. "This isn't the way Halloween should be." There should have been a constant knocking on the door, a parade of kids in costumes. She should have been listening to Charlie's laughter and chatter. "I planned to spend the night reading the tale of the headless horseman to Charlie."

"If you want," Roman said, "I can tell you a couple of scary stories."

"Made-up stories?"

"Not all of them."

"Here's one," she said. "Once upon a time, there was a lonely little girl who wanted a family more than anything. Her father had been stolen away—"

"Not by Gypsies, I hope. My people have taken a bum rap on a lot of kidnapping."

"Not Gypsies. Stolen away by a mad scientist. And she missed him…" Her voice trailed off as she blew out another candle. And another. There were only two remaining.

"What happened to the little girl?" Roman asked.

"She got what she wanted. A family of her own. Then she lost it. End of story. Scary, huh?"

He held the last ceramic pumpkin in his hand. The votive candle shimmered like the last star in a velvet night, and the light reflected softly on his handsome features. He seemed sympathetic and concerned about her.

She blew out the candle. Though there was still a glow from the kitchen, they were in the dark. The night was silent.

"Charlie's not going to leave you," he said. "He's just growing up."

"Too fast," she said. "This morning, he didn't want me to walk him to school. Tonight, he's gone with somebody else."

"Your son loves you."

She was glad for the darkness. Roman's simple statement affected her, and she could feel the beginning of tears behind her eyelids. "I should go to bed now."

"Alone?"

His voice held a teasing note, but she was still too embarrassed to joke about her behavior. "Definitely alone."

Feeling her way in the dark, she went toward the staircase. "Good night, Roman."

"Sweet dreams," he whispered as he watched her cross the room. Her white dress and blond hair made a pale shadow against the gloom. Their kisses still burned on his lips.

At the foot of the staircase, she turned. "I'm sorry about what happened earlier. When I came at you like that, you must have thought I was crazy."

Crazy and hot as a pistol. "Not at all."

"Thanks for understanding." She turned and continued up the stairs to her bedroom. "You're a good friend."

A *friend.* The word disgusted him. *Friends* didn't make

love. *Friends* didn't share the kind of passion that set the world on fire. It was hard to believe that he'd held this willing, sexy woman in his arms and hadn't made love to her. He'd wanted to. But there was no way he'd have sex with her here on the grounds of Legate where surveillance cameras were a way of life.

Though he wasn't sure Anya's cottage was bugged, it was best to assume that Big Brother was watching, and Roman wasn't about to give some watchdog a free show. When the time was right, he would make love to Anya in his own bed. Easily, he imagined her slender body stretched out on his black satin sheets with her long blond hair spread across his pillows. It would be slow and sensual and very, very hot.

Unspent passion surged through his blood. Damn it! He had to stop thinking like this or he'd never be able to walk across the grounds to the parking lot.

Roman turned on a lamp in the front room. Time to concentrate on something else, like his undercover operation. Thoughts of that tedious, ongoing investigative process were enough to throw cold water on any flame of desire.

Crossing the living room, he went to a small tidy desk near the door. Her backpack was on the floor beside it. Carefully, he eased open the single drawer, hoping he might find Charlie's medical records inside.

He rifled through the neatly labeled tabs. There was nothing marked ''Medical.'' Mostly, these were legal documents, tax information. He pulled out a folder marked ''Will.'' Here it was. The original signed copy of Jeremy's Last Will and Testament. An excellent find.

MORE THAN TWO WEEKS passed before Anya was alone with Roman again. She needed to go into San Francisco for her first language tutorial, and he insisted upon driving her.

At dusk, they exited the Legate compound with Roman behind the wheel of his Mercedes. An uncomfortable silence stretched between them. A thousand possible topics hung in the air. Unfortunately, 999 had to do with sex, and she didn't intend to go there.

She cleared her throat and said, "You really didn't have to drive me."

"Not a problem."

"I'm fully capable of finding my way around the big bad city all by myself."

"I like going into town," he said. "The Institute of International Languages isn't far from Chinatown, and I promised Charlie I'd find another puzzle box for him."

Her son always carried the little dragon from the first puzzle box in his pocket. For protection. "Charlie doesn't need any more presents."

Last week, Fredrick Slater gave him a brand-new, pocket-size computer with a multitude of global functions. It was very cool but much too expensive to be a toy. She worried about all this attention and all these gifts, fearful that her son would be spoiled rotten.

But Charlie wasn't front and center in her mind as she fidgeted in the leather bucket seat of Roman's speedy, smooth-riding vehicle. She was thinking about the man who sat beside her.

He tapped a button on the CD player and surround speakers serenaded them with the rich classical guitar of Andrés Segovia. The music masked the emptiness but didn't alter the charged atmosphere. After Halloween, there had been no more kissing. If they happened to touch, he flinched as if burned by a hot stove.

Anya told herself it was better this way. Roman was a

valued friend, a confidant and a great companion for her son. She didn't want to complicate that relationship with anything deeper. It had been a mistake to think she could have sex with him just for the fun of it.

Still, she couldn't help being attracted to him. On those occasions when he visited her cottage after work, he'd yank off his necktie and sprawl across her sofa with an unconscious grace that drove her wild. Just last night, while he sat on the edge of Charlie's bed and told him a bedtime story about a Gypsy prince, the glow from the bedside lamp outlined the classically handsome planes of Roman's face. She thought he was the most gorgeous creature she'd ever seen. Did she tell him? No! When he turned and caught her staring, she quickly looked away.

Clearly, she was a coward.

But there was another reason she didn't want to get too involved with Roman—something she dared not mention to him. As she delved deeper into Dr. Neville's research, she found more reasons to question the ethics of his project. Anya was beginning to suspect that all was not right at the Legate Corporation.

"So," Roman said, "your first language class."

"Yep." How much did he know about Neville's research? She hated to think he might condone these unprincipled experiments. But how could he be unaware?

"Seems like a strange time to start a semester," he said.

"This isn't a regular class," she informed him. "Apparently, I'm the only person interested in obscure Serbian and Bantu dialects. So this is a special tutorial."

"One-on-one instruction."

She nodded. "And, if I like the guy, I'll sign up for more."

He nodded.

So did she.

And Segovia played on the CD.

She allowed her gaze to slide toward him, looking for flaws. His profile wasn't perfect. There was a slight bump on his nose, as if it had been broken in a fight or an accident. His sculpted jawline had the beginnings of dark stubble. If she caressed his cheek, his skin would be scratchy. As if that mattered. She shouldn't even be thinking about touching him.

"Roman, have you been trying to avoid being alone with me?"

"No."

His response came too quickly. He was edgy. "Is something wrong?"

"Work problems," he said. "There's a lot going on at Legate."

"Do you want to share?"

"Not really."

She nudged a little harder. "Sometimes it's good to talk."

"Sometimes not." He raked a hand through his hair. "Here's the truth, Anya. I want to forget about Legate— the work, the projects, the hassles. I want to spend six months on a tropical island with nothing more to worry about than the turning of the tide."

"All by yourself?"

"You could come." A sly smile touched his lips. "But you have to promise you'd wear nothing more than a bikini top and a sarong."

"And what would you wear?"

"Not much," he said. "I want to feel the hot sun all over my body. To lie on a white sand beach cooled by whispering breezes through the palm fronds."

"This sounds like a very well-developed fantasy."

"You should know by now that I don't do things half-way."

That was certain. Once Roman got started on a course, there was no turning back. "What about Charlie? Could he come to your island?"

"Sure thing. And I'd teach him how to sail, how to fish and bodysurf. No genius instruction allowed."

"I'd like that," she said with heartfelt sincerity.

"Just you and me and Charlie," Roman said. "Walking barefoot on the shore. Splashing in sapphire waves. No responsibilities. No rush."

His vision of a verdant, tropical island was eclipsed by reality as they drove onto the Bay Bridge. It was a cold but strangely enchanting view. Below the bridge, the water was dark, mysterious and murky. On the opposite shore, the skyline of San Francisco shimmered through a light mist. As they came closer, she identified the piers on the Embarcadero, the distinctive shape of the Transamerica Pyramid and the skyscrapers of the financial district. "This is a far cry from the tropics."

"The opposite," he said. "Mobs of people. Constant frenzy. But I love the city, too. It has an intensity that makes me sit up and take notice."

The contrast defined him. Roman was a man who could happily play the role of Robinson Crusoe on a deserted island. But the sophistication and drama of San Francisco was an equally appropriate backdrop. "It must be the Gypsy in you," she said. "You could live anywhere."

"And never sink roots," he said.

"Always the bachelor."

In the city, he navigated the steep, complicated streets easily until they located the address for the Institute of International Languages a few blocks away from Union Square. The four-story brick building stood shoulder to shoulder with two others of differing architecture—typical of eclectic San Francisco.

Roman pulled up to the curb by the stoplight and peered over his shoulder. "I should go in with you," he said. "Let me find a real parking place."

"Don't be silly," she said. "I can manage."

"Which room is your tutorial in?"

She dug into her purse, looking for the slip of paper where her class confirmation was printed. "Room 228. Class is over at nine."

"If I can't find parking, I'll wait out here."

"Thanks, Roman."

As she left the car, she reached over and patted his cheek. His stubble felt like sexy sandpaper…if there was such a thing. She slammed the car door and strode toward the entrance.

The office foyer was charmingly aged with a dark wainscoting below cream-colored walls, but the halls were empty.

Anya took the open staircase to the second floor and knocked on the door of room 228. When no one answered, she entered the small classroom.

The heels of her loafers echoed as she crossed the wood floor. Was she the only person in this building? A shiver crawled up her spine. For a moment she wished she hadn't been so quick to send Roman away.

She placed her purse on one of the desk chairs and strolled around the room, glancing at the various posters of exotic locales. One was Aruba; it looked like the tropical island of Roman's fantasy.

The classroom door opened, and a man in a long trench coat entered. The collar was turned up, and she couldn't see his face. He was a stranger, but Anya knew him from his gait and his posture.

He closed the door and faced her. With a shrug, he removed his coat. "It's good to see you, sweetpea."

"Dad?"

Chapter Nine

In the North Beach area beyond Chinatown, Roman snagged a parking place on the street. He had another reason for being in the city tonight, and her name was Maureen.

Inside Corelli's restaurant, his red-haired CIA contact sat behind a red-and-white-checked tablecloth with her back to the wall. The neckline on her lavender blouse plunged nearly to her waist. Pinned to her shoulder was a matching silk flower. Maintaining their supposed "dating" cover, he leaned down to kiss her forehead before taking the chair opposite her.

"Were you followed?" she asked.

"Not on the way here from Legate. But when I'm in the city, it's tough to keep track of traffic." He sat and glanced at the menu. "Can we talk freely in here?"

"For a while."

The restaurant was more than half-full, and the chatter of other conversations would mask their own. Even an audio-surveillance expert would need a few minutes to set up listening equipment.

"I'll talk fast," he said.

She fiddled with the silk flower and smiled. "The recorder is on. Audio and video."

"An orchid-cam. Very nice."

She hunched her shoulder. "Talk to the flower."

He listed names and dates on a nefarious banking project in the South Pacific. His investigation into that project was the trigger that started him thinking about escapes to tropic isles.

Maureen leaned toward him. "I need a little more. Are you sure you can't check the computer records?"

Patiently, he explained, "You know I can't. If I open computer files, it could send up a red flag. Any computer search is my last resort before closing down this undercover operation."

Which he would be very glad to do. As soon as he figured out the motive for the explosion at Building Fourteen that killed Anya's husband. "Do you have anything for me on Jeremy's will?"

She placed an envelope on the small table. "This is your original. It's not a forgery. But forensic testing indicates that the paper on certain key pages came from a different stock."

Roman drew the logical conclusion. "Slater's lawyers inserted the section about Charlie attending the Legate school."

"Possibly. But it isn't the kind of proof that could stand up in court. There are too many other reasonable explanations for why the paper might be different."

Another dead end. He slipped the original into his suit coat pocket. "We need to talk about an escape strategy for Anya and Charlie."

"As far as we can tell, she's free to go."

Roman knew differently. He'd already obtained the medical records and verified the information Peter Bunch had given him. "It won't be that easy. Anya might have a hard time extricating her son."

"Why?" Maureen frowned. "Are you withholding information from me?"

"Turn off your flower, and I'll tell you."

Suddenly she sat up straight as though stung by a wasp.

"What's wrong?" he asked.

"I'm getting something."

She tilted her head and tapped at her earring which must have concealed a miniature transmitter. "I can't believe it," Roman muttered. "An orchid-cam on your shoulder and microphones in your jewelry. I suppose you've got a portable fax machine tucked inside your bra."

"Quiet," she snapped.

"What are you listening to? A radio tuned to the spook channel?"

"The guys doing surveillance on Anya." Maureen's eyes were deadly serious. "She's leaving the Institute of International Languages."

Damn! He'd sensed that he shouldn't leave Anya there alone. He should have followed his instincts and gone inside with her. "Where's she headed?"

"She's with a man."

"Who?" Roman was already standing.

"Wade Bouchard. Her father."

He pivoted and went to the door. When he exited into the evening dark, Maureen was at his side. Her hand was still on her ear. "They're headed toward Chinatown."

They were only a few blocks away. It was faster not to take his car. "Where in Chinatown?"

"California and Grant." She grabbed his arm before he could take off. "Slow down, Roman. My surveillance guys are on it. They want to tail Bouchard."

"Fine." He couldn't care less about Anya's father. "I'm going after her."

"Don't interfere." Her grip on his forearm tightened. "Don't get in the way."

"The hell I won't." He wouldn't stand by while the CIA used Anya for bait. "See ya."

With one sharp move, he broke away from her.

Maureen was a trained operative. If given half a chance, she might be able to slow him down with some clever martial arts moves—especially since he wouldn't strike back against a woman.

But Roman knew he was faster.

He took off into the night. His sprinter's reflexes served him well as he dodged pedestrians, leaped from the curbs and raced across streets ahead of the notoriously reckless San Francisco drivers.

He charged up the hill toward Chinatown. Damn it! What the hell did Wade Bouchard want with his daughter?

ANYA STRODE IN SILENCE beside her father. He'd aged considerably in the two years since she'd seen him. He seemed shorter, almost the same height as her. His gray hair had receded on his already high forehead, and his wrinkles had deepened to crevices. Only his lively blue eyes were the same. Wade Bouchard always seemed to be laughing at a punch line no one else heard.

"I love Chinatown." His expansive gesture took in the whole scene from the brightly lit store fronts at street level to the pagoda-style rooftops. It was a fascinating place where twin dragons coiled around the street lamps and lucky red predominated the colorful displays of trinkets. At the same time, there was a darkness around the edges, a hint of mystery. "Did I ever bring you here when you were a little girl?"

"I don't remember." But she doubted they'd made a trip to San Francisco. As a child, she surely would have recalled these exotic streets with two-and three-story buildings rising on either side, fascinating wares displayed in every shop window and signs written in English and Chinese. "We never took photos on vacations."

"I try not to be captured on film."

Always with the conspiracy theories! She didn't know whether to laugh or cry. Her father always had that effect on her.

"You could take Charlie here," she suggested. "He likes dragons."

"Does he now?"

She stepped aside for a small Asian woman pushing a huge cart filled with bright satiny material. Anya was reaching the end of her patience.

Wade paused at Wang Ho's Meat Market to examine the fresh squid. "Should I buy one? Squid is quite delicious if prepared with—"

"Great idea," she snapped. "We could have it for Thanksgiving."

"What?"

"Thanksgiving," she repeated. "It's next week, but why should you care? It's a family holiday—one of those occasions you never saw fit to celebrate."

"Turkey Day," he said. "A day of gluttony while the rest of the world is starving. Celebration? I think not."

"It's a family holiday," she repeated.

"The basis of this supposed holiday is the subjugation of the Native Americans who willingly offered their corn and their expertise to a band of uptight European colonists who—"

"Enough!" He really ticked her off. With him, nothing was ever fun. "Why did you arrange to see me?"

Wade glanced over his shoulder, looking for an invisible

enemy. "You've made a serious mistake, Anya. You never should have brought Charlie to Legate."

"Don't lecture me." He gave up that right when he abandoned her as a child. "Your opinion means zip to me."

"It's more than an opinion. Legate is evil. You're in danger. And I'm not the only one who thinks so."

"Who else? Some of your scientist buddies in SCAT?"

He gave her a sad smile. "I don't expect you to understand our mission and goals, but—"

"I know exactly what's going on." She refused to be drawn in to any of his conspiracy theories. "You've wasted your life tilting at windmills, and you hate the idea that your grandson might actually learn something at Legate. Charlie might accomplish something positive with his intelligence."

When he shook his head and walked a bit farther, she was tempted to let him go. She should turn her back, return to the Institute of International Languages and wait for Roman to pick her up at nine o'clock.

But what if her father was right? While she was studying Neville's files, Anya had the sense that some of Legate's policies were unethical. What if there was real danger?

Reluctantly, she fell into step beside him. "As long as you're here, you might as well tell me what you think."

"Are you familiar with the Topaku epidemic?" he asked.

"As a matter of fact, I am. An African village was tragically decimated by a virus. Thanks to Legate, the disease was halted before it spread."

"Thanks to Legate," he muttered. "If my epidemiology information is correct—and it usually is—the virus in question was of the Filoviridae group, similar to Ebola, which is animal-borne."

"Whoa, Dad. Give me the explanation in terms I can understand."

"The virus is spread through contact with livestock, birds or mosquitoes. Why did it suddenly appear in a geographically isolated village? And why did it go no farther?"

She'd read enough of the documents to have a fairly clear picture. "Legate developed a successful vaccine. They halted the spread."

"Of mosquitoes? Of birds?"

"What are you suggesting?" she asked.

"The epidemic was very neatly and precisely controlled because it was planned. Legate tested the efficiency of virus and vaccine at Topaku."

If true, Wade's accusation was horrific. Legate had experimented on human beings. "You think the villagers were purposely infected?"

"Yes," he said.

She couldn't believe him. "Based on what solid evidence?"

"If I knew, we wouldn't be standing here. My findings would be presented to the highest authority. Legate would be closed down."

"So this is just a theory of yours?"

He stopped at the mouth of an alley and turned toward her. His vivid blue eyes shimmered in his aged face. "If I had access to the Legate archives, I could prove these allegations. You could help me, Anya."

If his theory was true, she had a moral obligation to help him. If not, she could prove him wrong and he'd have to abandon this particular quest. "What do you want me to look for?"

"One particular memo. It's partially written in Bantu. The man who sent it is named Aringa."

She thought of the rows and rows of shelves in the archives and the surveillance cameras that would be watching her every move. "Finding one memo could be difficult."

"I'm sure it exists. And Legate keeps good records, including personal notes from scientists who worked on the virus and vaccine."

A truly horrible thought rose in her mind. Her husband had been a biochemist. This was his field. "According to your theory, was Jeremy involved?"

"No," Wade said quickly. "Jeremy was a good man. When he died, he was on the verge of severing his occasional employment with Legate."

But he never mentioned quitting to her. "How do you know what Jeremy planned? Did you talk to him?"

"I have my sources," he said evasively.

Though she knew better than to accept Wade's theories as truth, she asked, "What do you know about Roman? Can I trust him?"

Her father took a step into the alley. "Come with me, Anya. Everything will be revealed. You can help me. We'll work together."

Since childhood, she'd been waiting for this invitation from her father. *Come with me. Be a part of my life.* Every time he'd said goodbye, she wanted him to take her along. The abandoned little girl who still existed inside her was drawn to this man.

But she had to resist him. Anya was an adult with a child of her own. If she agreed to help Wade, she would surely be in jeopardy. And so would Charlie. "I can't work with you, Dad. I'll look for your supposed memo, but that's all."

"If you change your mind—"

"I won't," she said firmly. "I don't want to join your merry band of renegade scientists."

"Too bad. We could use someone with your language skills." He winked at her. "I'll be in touch."

With surprising agility, he turned and plunged deeper into the alley. He entered a nearly invisible door in the brick wall. He was gone.

A tiny voice within her whispered, "Bye, Daddy. I love you."

Unanswered words. *Love* had never been a part of Wade Bouchard's vocabulary. He devoted himself to saving the world and had no time to waste with a little girl who needed a father.

She wanted to go with him. Hesitantly, she stepped into the maw of the alley.

WHEN HE REACHED Grant Street, Roman slowed his pace. He was breathing so hard his chest ached. But not from exertion. Hell, he was in great shape; he could run for miles. It was fear that tightened his lungs. Inside his overcoat, sweat soaked through his shirt. What if he couldn't find her? *Concentrate. Look in all directions.*

At eight o'clock on a weeknight in November, the people on the sidewalks of Chinatown moved with purpose; they were headed home or finishing up errands. There weren't many sightseers. Street traffic progressed at a crawl. The day was winding down.

He peered into a souvenir shop crammed with trinkets and postcards. But Anya hadn't come here for the shopping. She wouldn't be browsing.

Squinting against the glare from neon signs in English and Chinese, he scanned the interiors of food markets, tea shops and bazaars, praying that she hadn't been lured into one of these buildings with the pagoda eaves. His gaze lifted to the lighted windows, two and three stories up. People disappeared in Chinatown. Behind the touristy facade, this was a dangerous place, teeming with intrigue.

Damn it, where was she? The thought of losing her scared him. He had to find her. When he did, there would be no more lies between them. He'd tell her the truth about everything—about Legate, the surveillance and Jeremy's death. No more lies and half-truths.

Amid the pedestrians on the opposite side of the street, he caught a glimpse of white-blond hair. Anya! He dashed across the street toward her.

Unmoving, she stood on the sidewalk outside an open-air market, staring into a cardboard box of gingerroot. Though she appeared to be alone, Roman couldn't be sure. Her father might be nearby. Or the CIA might have her under surveillance. And there was always the danger that Legate security was watching.

He should have been subtle in his approach, but he couldn't hold back. His instinct was to protect her, to gather her up and take her somewhere safe. He touched her arm, reassuring himself that she was real.

When she gazed up at him, her blue eyes were watery and confused. "Roman? What are you doing here?"

His usual glibness deserted him. Tongue-tied, he stared for a long moment before his brain kicked in. "Puzzle box," he said. Already, he'd broken his promise not to lie. "I was looking for a puzzle box for Charlie."

She nodded slowly. Her manner was strangely detached, preoccupied. What had she learned from her father? What had that old bastard told her? Roman suspected the worst. "What happened?" he asked.

"What do you mean?"

"To your class," he said. "At the institute."

"Nothing." She waved her hand in front of her face, brushing away the truth. "The teacher never showed.

Something must have come up. A family emergency or something. Then I came here, looking for you."

Like most people who were unaccustomed to lying, she'd said too much. "Let me see the class schedule they sent you."

She dug into her purse and produced the single sheet of paper marked with the logo for the Institute of International Languages. It listed the room number, the time, the date. The instructor's name was Chou Liu—the same name that was on the registry for the car Peter Bunch had emerged from.

Her tutorial lesson must have been a set-up. Roman should have known. He should have looked at this class receipt. "Were you able to verify this schedule?"

Her eyes flicked down then up. The corner of her mouth twitched. She was a pathetically bad liar. "The building was open. And I found somebody. And I'll have my class next week. Same time."

And meet with her father again? Not if Roman could help it. "Next time, I'll come inside with you," he said. "To make sure your professor is there."

She swallowed hard and forced a smile. "You don't have to. It's okay. Really."

Why wasn't she telling the truth? Why the hell were they both lying to each other? "It's chilly out here. Let's get moving."

He tucked her hand under his arm and backtracked along the streets that led to his car. As they walked, a sense of danger dogged their footsteps. He could feel the eyes of strangers who watched from the shadows. Their ears listened. They were everywhere. The CIA. Legate security. The fanatics in SCAT.

Roman wished he had a gun to protect her. When he

risked his own skin, he wasn't afraid. Having Anya with him made everything different.

He felt her shiver, and he knew it wasn't from the night chill. She was scared, too.

"You're not alone," he reassured her.

"Well, of course not. You're with me."

"You'll never be alone again."

He would convince her to trust him. It was time for all the lies to end.

Outside the Italian restaurant in North Beach, he spotted Maureen, standing at a bus stop. She looked angry, but that was too damned bad. The CIA could go to hell. He'd fed them enough information. This undercover operation was over as soon as Anya and Charlie were safely gone from Legate.

Inside his car with the doors locked, he felt more secure. Starting tomorrow, he'd carry his 9mm Smith & Wesson in his glove compartment. "Hungry?"

"I should be," she said. "But I'm not."

He understood. Deceit took a lot of concentration. There wasn't much room left for normal appetites.

"I'm starved," he said. "We'll stop at my house for something to eat."

"I should get back to Charlie."

"Your mother is with him. She's already planning to spend the night at your cottage."

"But I want to be there."

"You'll be home soon enough," he promised.

If he was going to reveal his whole complicated story, he intended to do it right. They'd sit down and talk like civilized human beings.

She'd be angry. He was sure of that. But she might also forgive him. And he needed her absolution. When all was said and done, he could face her with a clean slate. Not as her late husband's best friend. Not as an official of Legate. Or an undercover operative.

He wanted her to see him as a man who cared deeply about her and her son. A man who wanted to be more than just a friend.

Chapter Ten

When Roman brought her into his house, Anya had the sense that she was more a prisoner than a guest. If her father's accusations about Legate were true, Roman was surely culpable. But had he known the truth about the To-paku epidemic? Had he allowed those villagers to die?

Somehow, she couldn't believe it. Roman might be an arrogant womanizer with a lot of secrets, but he wasn't a monster.

In the kitchen, he tossed his car keys on the countertop and kept walking. "Come with me."

She balked. "Where?"

"My bedroom."

All too well, she remembered that den of seduction with the lavish bed and the sumptuous red walls. Though it seemed the height of naïveté to waltz into his lair, Roman hadn't been sending out his usual seductive vibes. On the drive here, he spoke very little and seemed lost in his own thoughts. Anya followed him up the staircase.

She heard him command, "Computer on."

"Welcome home, Roman," the sultry computer voice whispered. "It's 8:53."

"Classical music," he said. "Personal mix."

A violin concerto played. Anya couldn't identify the piece but thought it might be Mozart.

Roman sloughed off his camel coat and tossed it carelessly over his desk chair. "I had a reason for bringing you here," he said. "This room is the only place I can be sure we're not under surveillance. No one can see us here. No one can eavesdrop."

She didn't understand. "Why would anyone want to listen to us?"

"Cameras and microphones are everywhere. Like at Legate. You can't make a move without someone watching, listening."

"It's just normal security," she said.

"There's nothing normal about it." His voice was bitter. "In the future, you should assume that you're under constant surveillance."

"Even in my cottage?"

"It's possible."

She was horrified. In the supposed privacy of her own home, she let down her guard. Home was the place where she talked to herself and sang along with the radio. Sometimes she danced. Sometimes she wept. And someone was watching her? The idea that she'd been observed—studied like a paramecium under a microscope—was dehumanizing, humiliating. "Why didn't you tell me?"

"I couldn't take the chance that you'd behave in an unnatural manner."

"Unnatural how?"

"You're the most straightforward woman I've ever known. Don't get me wrong. That's a positive trait." He gave her a quick smile. "An endearing trait."

"Thanks, I think."

"But in this situation, honesty isn't a plus. The things

I'm about to tell you have to remain a closely guarded secret. You can't let anyone know.''

''Why not?''

''Because if you talk, you're in danger.'' As he crossed the room toward the bed, he pointed toward the modular sofa and chair in between the sleeping area and the desk. ''You might want to sit down. This is a long story.''

Nervously, she sat. Her gaze drifted toward the bed. The satin duvet shone enticingly in the soft lamplight. Though she could feel her internal temperature rising, she didn't remove her black pea coat. She wanted that extra layer of protection.

In a wall unit beside his bed was a wet bar. Roman asked, ''Can I get you something to drink?''

''Water.''

He opened the refrigerator and took out a bottled water for her while he poured himself a glass of wine. His actions seemed perfectly normal for a man coming home after a long day. And yet, she sensed an overriding tension in the way he moved as he came toward her.

He placed her water bottle on the coffee table, removed his suit jacket and sat beside her. ''You could lose the coat,'' he said.

''I'm fine.''

''It looks like you're ready to race out the door at any given second.''

''Maybe I am.'' Her legs, in black denim slacks, crossed one over the other. Her dangling foot swung nervously to and fro. ''Go ahead, Roman. We don't have all night.''

He stretched out his long legs and rested his feet on the coffee table. ''It was over a year ago that I became aware of a problem at Legate. They were playing fast and loose with some federal regulations on offshore banking for an emerging nation in Central America. I started looking into it.''

His tone was utterly calm as though he was reciting a bedtime story for Charlie. But she had a feeling this tale wouldn't end with ''and they lived happily ever after.''

''I found evidence of criminal dealings,'' he said.

''At Legate?''

He nodded. ''Until that time, I was unconcerned with the interior working of our various projects. My job was to set goals and budgets, to meet schedules and handle personnel problems. I liked to think of myself as a motivator, someone who got from point A to point B without worrying about the path in between.''

As in the Topaku epidemic? ''So you didn't know the details?''

''I chose not to know.'' Roman wasn't proud of his behavior. For years, he kept his blinders on. ''When I first came to Legate, I'm certain there was nothing illegal or immoral going on.''

That was almost nine years ago. He was a young man in his twenties, full of enthusiasm and intoxicated with the power of his position—administrator of an international think tank. ''I was seduced.''

''In what sense?'' she asked.

His gesture encompassed the lavish bedroom that took up the entire top floor of his house. ''Obviously, I was very well paid.''

His lifestyle went far beyond anything he had ever hoped to achieve. On a daily basis, he associated with brilliant and powerful individuals. His name was on the guest list at important events. Women threw themselves at his feet. It was exciting to live in the fast lane.

''I can't blame anyone else. I was a willing recruit for Slater, and I truly believed Legate was a force for good, capable of taking on the problems of the world and solving them.''

''But you were mistaken?''

''Yes,'' he said.

''How did you find out?''

When he looked at her, his dark eyes were tortured. ''The deeper I looked into Legate projects, the more unethical procedures I found. Corporations were destroyed in hostile takeovers. Scientific discoveries were manipulated.''

Anya didn't understand. ''Why?''

''You know the Legate motto.''

''For The Greater Good,'' she said.

''No matter who gets trampled along the way. The greater good means the enrichment and entertainment of Fredrick Slater. After I finally figured that out, I couldn't play along anymore. I contacted the CIA.''

Her breath caught in the back of her throat. The CIA? The danger her father suggested was becoming very real. And she was caught in the middle of it, trapped in a web of conspiracies.

Roman continued. ''I started feeding information to the CIA. Working undercover.''

''You're a spy?''

''Nothing so dramatic. I'm just a guy who's finally trying to do the right thing. I didn't know how dangerous this was until…'' He set down his wineglass, reached over and gently took her hand. ''Until Jeremy was killed.''

She heard the words, but they didn't register. *Jeremy. Was. Killed.* A terrible calm settled over her. Perhaps she'd always known…. ''Are you saying that my husband's death was not an accident?''

''I was there, Anya. I had just left his office. I heard three explosions in rapid succession. Boom. Boom. Boom.

That wasn't a gas main exploding. It was a carefully trig-
gered explosion."

"But there was an investigation."

"A cover-up," Roman said.

"And you have proof?"

"Not yet. That's why I've stayed at Legate, working
undercover. I couldn't leave until I knew the whole truth
about Jeremy's murder."

Slowly and deliberately, she reclaimed her hand and
rested it upon her thigh. She was hot, sweating. Clumsily,
she removed her jacket and straightened her pale turquoise
blouse. Every detail in the room became vividly clear. She
was aware of her heart beating and a paralyzing tension in
every muscle—aware that she was drifting into a state that
resembled shock. *Jeremy was murdered.* "Was it because
of the project he was working on?"

"No," Roman said. "There were four scientists killed
in the explosion. None of them were involved in complex
research."

"All biochemists?"

"Yes."

"The Topaku epidemic," she said.

"Why the hell does everyone keep bringing that up?
You've seen the information. Legate behaved in a responsible manner. Their efforts prevented the spread of a potential plague."

"Unless they were responsible for the virus in the first
place. Unless they started the infection."

"Why would you think that?"

Because her father had told her. Wade Bouchard's wild
theory might be true. "If one of those murdered scientists
knew or suspected that Legate was responsible for killing
the people in that village, it's a motive for murder."

"None of them worked directly on Topaku," he said.

"But tomorrow I'll see if they were tangentially connected."

"Why not now? You've got the supercomputer."

"I can't use it," he said with obvious frustration. "If I check into those files, Slater can trace the contact back to me."

She lifted the water bottle to her lips and took a long pull. Her fingers trembled as she placed the bottle back on the coffee table. *Jeremy was murdered.* The Legate Corporation had torn her husband away from her and left her son without a father.

"Charlie," she whispered. "Oh, my God. Charlie."

She had to get him away from here before anything else happened. "How could you let me bring my son to this terrible place?"

"I advised against it. Don't you remember?"

"You should have been more direct."

"I couldn't tell you my suspicions. If you knew, you'd be in certain danger."

"And now?" A burst of anger exploded behind her eyes. How could this happen? "Now I'm in danger. My son is in danger."

"No," he said. "Slater would never do anything to harm Charlie."

"Except kill his father." She drew back her hand and slapped his face. "Damn you, Roman."

The sting of contact surprised her. But she raised her hand to strike again. He caught her wrist. "I'm on your side."

"You've done nothing but lie to me."

She surged to her feet and wrenched away from him. A terrible pain burned inside her. Hurt and angry, she wanted to scream. To tear apart his expensive house.

She wanted to run. But where would she go? There was

no escape. The pressure inside her built to an unbearable level.

Roman came to her, stood beside her. "Anya, I'm sorry."

"Don't touch me."

She stormed away from him. Toward the bed. No, not the bed. She paced back toward the computer. Not that way, either. Oh, God! How could this be true?

Her husband was killed. She was bereft, alone. Her son, her baby, was robbed of his father.

A guttural sob clawed up her throat, and she couldn't hold it back. The air exploded from her lungs in an unintelligible cry. Tears burst from her eyes. Streaming rivulets coursed down her cheeks. The dam had broken. A fury of emotion battered her, and she sank to her knees, helpless to stop the tide of grief and rage. Murdered!

In sheer frustration, she threw back her head and screamed like a wounded animal. Her eyelids squeezed shut, and she slumped over.

When Roman touched her back, she cringed. "Leave me alone."

But he stayed beside her on the floor. He patted her shoulder.

"I said go!" She rose up on her knees and shoved at his chest. There was no comfort for her, no way to stop this spew of emotions. It felt like the moment when she first heard of Jeremy's death…like he'd been killed all over again.

Sobbing uncontrollably, she fell against Roman. And she wept until her eyes ran dry of tears. Residual shudders wracked her body. She felt him lifting her off her feet, carrying her.

"You need to sleep now," he said as he placed her on

the bed. ''I'll call your mother and tell her you won't be home until tomorrow.''

''But Charlie—''

''He'll be fine.''

She should have objected, demanded to be taken home. To the cottage? Where she'd be watched?

They'd killed her husband. They might as well kill her, too. Was that the plan? To murder the parents and take Charlie? Her darling son would be turned into an instrument of evil. His intelligence would be used to destroy.

It was too terrible to imagine. She closed her eyelids and allowed darkness to overwhelm her.

Chapter Eleven

Anya woke with a start. Blinking, she peered into the shadows of the unfamiliar bedroom—a huge, open space that was plush and luxurious. Roman's bedroom.

Thoughts pieced together like an emotional mosaic in her mind. Sorrow. Rage. Frustration.

She'd been crying. Her eyes still stung from the nearly hysterical outpouring of tears. Jeremy had been murdered. Damn the Legate Corporation and all it stood for…except Roman. He worked for the CIA. It all seemed impossible and unreal.

"Roman?" She spoke into the darkness. "Are you here?"

There was a rustling from across the room. He said, "Computer, morning light."

A gradual pinkish glow flushed two walls of the bedroom. Subtle sounds accompanied the illusion of daybreak. She heard the soft whisper of wind through conifers and the quiet chirping of sparrows. It was like sunrise in the mountains. If only she were back in Denver and none of this had ever happened. If only she hadn't come to Legate.

"What time is it?" she asked.

He mumbled, "Computer, time."

The sultry computer voice answered, "Eleven thirty-seven."

Though Anya had only slept for a couple of hours, Anya felt somehow refreshed as though she'd been cleansed by finally knowing the truth. The violent storm of discovery had passed. She knew the worst and now had to deal with the aftermath.

"How are you feeling?" Roman asked as he approached the bed.

"Better."

She was well enough to notice that he wore only silky black pajama bottoms and an open robe—kind of a Ninja-looking outfit. Under the sheets, she was still fully clothed, except for her shoes.

He stood at the end of the bed. "Can I bring you anything?"

"A new life?" Somewhere in the back of her mind, she'd always suspected that her husband's death wasn't an accident. "I'm glad I know the real story."

"The truth is dangerous," he said. "Remember, Anya. You can't tell anyone."

"You said that before, and I still don't understand why I can't say anything. At the very least, I should talk to the police."

"The same police who said the explosion was an accident?"

He had a point. If the police had been duped before into believing that the explosion was an accident, they had no reason to listen to her. "There must be somebody I can go to. Slater can't get away with murder."

"He's a vindictive bastard. Don't even think about threatening him."

"Can I think about shoving him off a cliff? Mowing him down with an AK-47?"

"Such nasty fantasies from such a beautiful woman." He sat on the bed beside her. "Are you ready for another dose of truth?"

She groaned. Normally, she didn't wake up quickly no matter how many stereophonic birds were twittering. "I don't want to hear any more bad news, not until I've had coffee."

"Computer, coffee," he said.

"You're kidding, right?"

"Not at all. The computer is electronically connected to everything in this room. She sends a signal over to the coffeemaker in the wet bar."

"No wonder you've never married," she said. "All the basic needs are taken care of by a computer."

"Not *all* my needs," he said.

His eyes were hot. Smoldering, in fact.

She was amazed that he could go from a dead sleep to dead sexy in a couple of minutes. Men truly were different from women.

It occurred to her that she ought to get out of his bed. Lounging here in opulent splendor might give him the wrong impression. Like what? That she wanted to make love? Maybe she did.

Anya stole a glance at the strong, handsome man who was less than an arm's length away. She'd been right when she guessed that Roman had been keeping things from her. My God, what secrets! He worked for the CIA.

Now that he had finally told her the truth, she could trust him. She plumped up the pillows against the headboard, creating a nest where she could sit upright and pretend to be alert. "You said there was something else you needed to tell me."

"Nothing bad," he said.

She didn't think any revelation could be worse than what he'd told her last night. "Go ahead."

"I want you to think back. To the day when Jeremy first introduced us. It was autumn. The trees were turning. We were at a bistro in Denver."

"I remember." It was seven years ago, before she and Jeremy were married, before Charlie was born. "He'd talked so much about you. Roman this. And Roman that. You were like a big brother to him."

"We were always a little competitive. And I'm not bragging when I say I usually won. I was bigger and stronger and a hell of a lot more aggressive. But on that day, at that bistro in Denver, I was jealous of Jeremy."

"Why?"

"Because of you. From the first time I saw you, I admired the way you looked, the way the sun caught in your hair and that sly smile you have when you're amused. I liked your wit. Your spirit. I wished with all my heart that I'd seen you first."

Her jaw fell open. This wasn't what she had expected.

He reached toward her and lightly caressed her cheek. "Of course, I'll always be your friend. But here's the simple truth—I want more, Anya. I want to be your lover."

She should have said something, but all she could manage was a strangled noise in the back of her throat.

When she had considered making love with him, she wanted an affair, a fling. Nothing deep and meaningful. Just fun. All of a sudden, Roman was turning sensitive and… lovable.

"Believe me," he said. "You're the only woman I've ever met who I can imagine staying with for any length of time."

"No, no." She shook her head. "This can't be. You're

Roman Alexander, confirmed bachelor and man-about-town.''

''Maybe it's time for a new role. Roman Alexander, family man.''

But she wasn't ready to fall in love. Not with him. Not with anyone. She needed more time. ''Of course, I like you Roman, but—''

''Stop right there.'' He placed his finger across her lips. ''If you tell me again that we're such good friends, I'll shoot myself.''

''What's wrong with—''

''Don't think about what you ought to say. Don't tell me what's proper and sensible. Tell me the truth. Tell me what's in your heart. Think of how you feel when we touch.''

Her sensory memory kicked in. She remembered the pure, mindless delight of his embraces. A sweet trembling glimmered through her, making the hairs on her arms stand up. He was good—a really good kisser.

If she allowed her thoughts to linger on this rose-strewn path, she'd be tearing off her clothes in a matter of seconds. ''Is that coffee ready?''

When he went to the wet bar and filled two mugs, she ordered her brain to regroup. Just because she'd slept in his bed didn't mean she'd…sleep with him. ''Only a couple of hours ago, I learned that my husband was murdered. I found out that Fredrick Slater—the man who should be my son's benefactor—is a disgusting, corrupt bastard. I have a great deal to think about. Like, how am I going to leave Legate? How will I explain to Charlie? He loves the school. There's a lot for me to figure out.''

He handed her a mug. The fragrance of the freshly brewed coffee seemed familiar and reassuring.

"But right now," he said, "you and I are in my bedroom. Alone."

"Drinking coffee." She took a taste. "Delicious. Does Ms. Computer cook?"

"Not yet, but I'm working on a program."

When he reached over to place his mug on the bedside table, his robe gaped open. A sprinkle of hair covered his muscular chest, then arrowed down toward the drawstring on his black silk pajama bottoms.

Her fingers itched, wanting to touch him, to revel in the texture of his shiny, black chest hair. Why shouldn't she give in to the urge?

No! Not yet!

"Roman, how am I going to get away from Legate with Charlie?"

"You have a contract with an escape clause," he said. "My CIA contact advises me that you ought to be able to leave as soon as you're ready."

But she sensed a hesitation on his part. "You don't believe it'll be that easy."

"I want you to wait for a few days, to make sure there's an escape strategy in place."

"A strategy?" That sounded very military—like something that involved the mobilization of tanks and Hummers. "What are you talking about?"

"You might want to have a lawyer with you," he said. "Possibly, you should leave first and tell Slater after you're gone."

"That sounds good to me. I've never been big on confrontations." She nodded. "I could do it tonight. I'll throw Charlie in the back of the minivan and drive away. When we're back in Denver, I'll call Slater. There won't be anything he can do about it."

"Patience, Anya."

"What's the problem?"

"Slater went to a lot of trouble to bring you here. He won't stand idly by while you pack up and run."

"What choice does he have?"

"Plenty," Roman said. "You've seen the security at Legate. They're not only well armed, but they're trained. This is an elite force of commandos. They have high-tech weaponry at their disposal, tracking devices, choppers. You wouldn't get ten miles without—"

"Hold it!" She couldn't believe Slater would deploy the troops. "The last time I checked, this was still America. There are laws against holding somebody against their will."

"Fredrick Slater is on a first-name basis with four Supreme Court justices. He dines regularly with the California governor. He knows the laws, knows the people who wrote them and knows how to change them."

It all came down to a chilling equation: Slater had power. She didn't. "You're scaring me, Roman."

"You need to be scared. You need to consider every worst-case scenario. This isn't a time when you can be impulsive or reckless."

"I need to be undercover," she said. "Like you."

"Right."

But she wasn't good at hiding her feelings. Anya couldn't keep a secret for five minutes. She couldn't even keep the presents hidden before Christmas morning.

And they weren't talking about Santa Claus. They weren't playing games. These were the highest stakes. Her freedom. The safety of her child. If she failed, she might lose everything.

Her fears multiplied. Her hands began to shake, and she set down her coffee cup. "I can't do this. How can I look Slater in the eye without spitting?"

"I'll help you."

"You can't be with me all the time." She was up on her knees in the middle of his bed. "How long will it take to come up with—what did you call it?—an escape strategy?"

"A couple of days. Maybe a week. Maybe more."

She shook her head. "I can't. I've never been able to fake it."

He had the audacity to chuckle. "I always knew that about you."

"Don't start talking about sex again." She jabbed a finger at him. "Just don't."

"Talk isn't what I had in mind."

In one swift move, he was up on the bed, kneeling opposite her, so close that she could feel the warmth radiating from his hard, virile body. If she inched forward, ever so slightly, the tips of her breasts would rub against his chest. If she reached out…

"Anya," he said gently. "I told you the truth about how I feel. Now it's your turn."

"I can't think about this now."

He leaned down and kissed her cheek. "Now might be the only time we have."

As she gazed up into his eyes, he seemed to absorb her fear. Though he'd lied to her, he had a good reason. And he was telling the truth now. Roman was a good man, had always been there for her.

But she didn't know how she really felt about him. "When Jeremy died, my heart was torn into a million pieces. My life was devastated. Roman, I can't risk falling in love again."

"Tell me how you feel about me. The truth."

"Can't we just—"

"Try," he urged.

"*Attraction* is too tame a word." The energy that crackled between them was a force of nature as powerful as a lightning bolt. "When you kiss me, it's like nothing I've ever experienced before."

"Like this?"

He held her face in both of his hands. His lips claimed hers with a demanding pressure as though he expected something in return, something she was glad to give.

A soft moan escaped her lips as her resistance crumbled to dust. She couldn't hold back. Not for one more second.

Her hands slipped inside his robe and climbed his hair-roughened chest. When she splayed her fingers and stroked, his muscles twitched and trembled at her touch.

His hands broke away from her face, but his gaze held her. The light in his tawny-brown eyes was a promise and a challenge as he positioned her hands around his neck.

Their bodies had not yet made contact, and the anticipation of finally joining with him created an unbearable yearning within her.

"Should I stop?" he asked.

"No."

"Are you sure?"

"Make love to me, Roman."

He encircled her with his arms and crushed her against his chest. He kissed her, hard and deep. His hands cupped her buttocks and held her tight against his long, hot erection. She ground her pelvis against him. His arousal fanned the heat of her passion. No holding back.

All thoughts vanished. All her worries were gone. There was only this moment—this precious time when sensual heat consumed her body. She needed him.

With his mouth joined to hers, he lowered her onto the sheets. With his knee, he parted her thighs. With his hand, he stroked and manipulated her with a rhythm that drove her wild.

She clung to him. His touches and kisses built a frenzy inside her. She was hot and wet, ready for him. More than ready.

But Roman took his time. A master of seduction, every move he made was skilled. He glided her blouse over her head, unfastened her bra. He teased her nipples with light flicks, then he suckled.

And she moaned with pleasure. She gave herself completely to him, followed his guidance. He was the choreographer in this sensuous ballet. He showed her the moves, and she'd never before felt so competent in the art of lovemaking.

Without groping or clumsiness, they were naked, exploring each other's bodies with delicate strokes that became gradually more intense until he sheathed himself in a condom and entered her, dominated her, overwhelmed her.

She heard herself cry out. Her trembling exploded in a crescendo. Wave after wave. Again and again. Until she was soaring, higher than an eagle could fly. She was up where the air was thin and the light was pure.

His body went rigid. He took his own pleasure in throbbing release, then collapsed on the bed beside her, gasping.

She closed her eyes and savored the aftershocks. Total ecstasy. Utter pleasure. She had a brand-new definition of *fun*. Feeling giddy, she grinned.

Though she had a million things to worry about, she savored this moment. She almost felt…happy.

With a lazy sigh, she turned toward him. He was so perfectly handsome. She traced the line of his nose with her fingertip. "Has this been broken?"

"Twice."

"How?"

"Once playing basketball. Once in a fight."

She suspected he was a good fighter—tough, strong and aggressive. "Let me guess. Were you fighting over a girl?"

"Nothing so romantic," he said. "The other guy smashed me in the face with a chair."

She shuddered. "Men are so weird. I hope Charlie doesn't get in fights."

"I hope he does." Roman propped himself on his elbow and gazed at her. "No matter how smart he is, it's important for him to be a regular guy."

For a moment, she lost herself in the glow from his eyes, the stunning warmth that radiated from him. Then she grinned again. "And how does one become a regular guy?"

"Burping contests," he said. "Scratching, swearing, howling at the moon."

"Charming."

He leaned down to kiss her forehead. "I'm starved. Do you want anything to eat?"

"Absolutely."

"This means I have to go down to the kitchen." He climbed out of bed. "But I'll be back."

He didn't bother with clothes. As he crossed the bedroom with a confident strut, she thoroughly appreciated the view of his muscular legs, his high butt and wide shoulders. He was magnificent.

Contented, she lay back on the black satin pillows. Making love had replenished her spirit and given her confidence. She could deal with Legate and Slater. Roman wouldn't let anything bad happen to her. He'd told her the truth about everything, and she could trust him.

When he came back up here, she'd tell him about meeting her father in San Francisco. That bit of information might be useful.

She closed her eyes and listened to the chirping birdsongs which had become rather annoying. "Computer, stop twittering," she said.

But her voice had no effect. Ms. Computer only responded to Roman.

Anya sat up and glared at the plasma screen. Surely there was some kind of manual control. Wrapping herself in Roman's robe, she crossed the bedroom to the keyboard. She touched the Escape key. Nothing happened. Maybe there was an instruction manual in the file drawer.

She pulled it open. The first file was labeled with her name. Interesting.

Though it might be considered spying to go through his files without permission, absolute trust meant they had no secrets. She flipped open the folder. Inside were medical records for herself and Jeremy. And for Charlie. Why did Roman have this information?

She couldn't think of a logical reason. It was obvious that he was still hiding something from her. The realization cut like a knife through her contentment. She'd been too quick to believe him. How much of what he'd told her was a lie?

Chapter Twelve

Six days later, Anya confronted Roman. They were, once again, in his bedroom. Once again, her mother was spending the night with Charlie while Anya supposedly attended her language seminar in San Francisco.

Though they had only been in his house for a few moments, Roman already had her on the bed. Not that Anya was an unwilling participant.

Clutching her half-unbuttoned blouse, she called a halt. "There's something I have to say."

Indulgently, he fell back on the duvet, giving her a little room. "Can you tell me in three-word sentences?"

"I hate secrecy."

"But you're doing very well at it," he said. "I've hardly noticed a difference in your behavior."

"Except that I dress in my closet at home," she muttered. No way would she give the possible secret cameras a peep show.

"What else?" he asked.

"Are you lying?" she asked in three words. She was thinking of the medical records she'd seen in his desk drawer. "Still."

"Are you?"

As he regarded her with eyebrows raised, she felt guilty.

She still hadn't mentioned the meeting with her father last week. Since she wasn't quite ready to broach that topic, she turned to another subject, something else that had been bothering her. "Do you remember Neville's research paper? The study on in vitro bonding?"

"What about it?"

"It's unethical, and I think it should be stopped."

"Give me the details."

"Neville has done a long-term psychological study of parents who underwent in vitro fertilization at the Legate clinic. The test group isn't large. Only twenty-seven couples." She frowned. "I wonder why Jeremy and I weren't included."

"Because Jeremy worked here as a consultant," Roman said. "It's policy not to involve employees in surveys or studies."

"Probably a good policy. An employee might not be as forthcoming as an outsider."

"Also, it's a subtle but effective way to maintain secrecy. The right hand never knows what the left is doing," he said. "What were Neville's conclusions?"

"His assumption was that parents who had struggled to conceive a child would bond more intensely with their babies. And he discovered high levels of anxiety, fear and guilt in the first few months. Especially among the mothers."

"I understand the anxiety and fear," Roman said. "Why guilt?"

"I can tell you that from my own experience." She edged her way off the bed. "When I couldn't get pregnant, I felt like it was my fault. Even though the data showed the likely reason was Jeremy's low sperm count, it seemed like there was something wrong with me. That I didn't deserve a baby."

"Fairly irrational."

She nodded. "Being pregnant isn't a rational process. Your hormones are going crazy, and your body is doing this amazing thing, creating life."

"I never saw you when you were pregnant," Roman said. "I assume you were radiant."

"Sure, when I didn't have morning sickness, painfully sensitive breasts and swollen feet." She left his bed and went to the wet bar where she rummaged through the refrigerator until she found a pint-size bottle of orange juice.

"I must be missing something," Roman said. "I don't see why Neville's research is unethical."

"He lied." She yanked the cap off the orange juice. Every time she thought about this experiment, she was outraged. "Half of these couples were able to get pregnant. The other half weren't, and Legate arranged for them to adopt an infant."

Roman nodded. "And?"

"With four of the adopting couples, Neville used surrogate mothers. They were implanted with the egg or sperm of the original couple who hadn't conceived." She took a long swig of her orange juice. "And he didn't tell them."

Roman clarified. "They didn't know that their supposedly adopted child was actually part of their DNA."

"In the name of experimentation, Neville kept that knowledge from them. He wanted to see if those parents—who were unaware of their DNA connection to the child—bonded differently."

"Did they?"

"Who cares?" She paced across the vast expanse of his bedroom. "That's a terrible thing to do. Not to tell a parent the truth about their kid? It's cruel. Somebody should lock up Neville and throw away the key."

"I'm with you on that," Roman said. "I'd like to see

Neville in jail with his necktie and pocket handkerchief matching an orange jumpsuit.''

"You're not taking this seriously," she said.

"Did Neville actually publish his results on this genetic-bonding study?"

"Partially. He kept the part about his lying separate. I found it in the archives."

"Get me your data," Roman said. "I'll pass it along to the proper authorities."

"The CIA?"

"Better than that," he said. "We'll turn over the data to the ethics board of the American Psychiatric Association. Neville will be disgraced in front of his peers."

Somewhat mollified, she returned to his bed. "I told you what was bothering me. Is there something you want to tell me about?"

"Quid pro quo?"

She nodded. "I give you the truth in exchange for truth from you."

"You're on." He rose from the bed and went to his desk where he pulled open his file drawer. When he returned, he held a several-page-long document, which he dropped on the bed beside her. "Jeremy's Last Will and Testament."

"Where did you get this?"

"I took it from your desk," he said. "I suspected a forgery, and I gave it to the CIA for testing."

Her fingers glided across the top sheet. "What did the CIA find?"

"The signature is Jeremy's. But there's evidence that some of the pages might have come from a different stock."

"The pages dealing with putting Charlie in the Legate school?"

Roman nodded. "Unfortunately, it's not enough evidence to invalidate the will."

"But it's enough for me."

A calm settled over her as one more piece of the puzzle fell into place. Jeremy hadn't been keeping secrets. He hadn't made plans for Charlie's future without talking to her.

She'd been duped by a phony legal document. She should have been incensed. Angry at Legate. Angry at Roman for stealing the will.

Instead, she felt vindicated. Her relationship with Jeremy had been honest and aboveboard. This knowledge meant more to her than she could express in words. She leaped into Roman's arms and held on tight. "Thank you."

He held her close. The room was silent except for a soft hum from the computer.

"Quid pro quo," he said. "Your turn."

She might have told him about her father. In exchange, she might have demanded to know why he had those medical records in his file. But she was sure there was a simple explanation, and she didn't want to break the mood. "There's nothing else I want to know right now."

She abandoned all other questions and allowed her mind to shut down. All she wanted tonight was to lose herself completely in passion.

"Turkey Day!" Charlie's ear-splitting yell ricocheted off the walls of Anya's minivan.

In the passenger seat, Roman turned around to look at the almost-six-year-old boy who was brimming with excitement. "And what happens on Turkey Day?"

"We eat." Charlie waved his arms. "Till our intestines explode."

Behind the wheel, Anya glanced worriedly in the rearview mirror. "Let's think about calming down, Charlie. We're almost at your grandmother's house."

"I'm going to eat two drumsticks and a whole pumpkin pie," he announced.

"Not if I get there first," Roman said.

"I can eat more than you." Charlie scowled at him. "I can eat more than a horse."

"Yeah? Well, I can eat more than an elephant."

Charlie bared his teeth. "I can eat more than T-Rex—"

"Gentlemen," Anya interrupted. "This is not a pig-out contest. We're supposed to be giving thanks."

"Thanks for the eats," Charlie said. "Turkey Day!"

Roman gave him a wink and faced forward. Though he wasn't particularly thrilled about spending an afternoon at Claudette's home in the North Beach area of San Francisco, he enjoyed being part of this little group. The new role suited him. Roman Alexander, family man.

Making love to Anya changed him in ways he hadn't anticipated. He was still tearing away at the mysteries surrounding Legate and was still very much aware of the potential for danger, but he also found himself smiling at odd moments, even when he was alone.

For a long time, he'd concentrated on revenge for Jeremy's murder. Now Roman's goals were bigger. He wanted to take care of Jeremy's family—Anya and Charlie. He'd help them heal. Not that he was being utterly altruistic. Roman had a lot to gain in this process.

When Anya pulled into the narrow driveway outside her mother's house, Charlie threw off his seat belt, flung open the van door and leaped out. "Turkey Day!"

"I don't know what's gotten into him," Anya muttered. "He's beastly."

"He's just acting like a kid." Roman touched her cheek

and ran his thumb across her lips. "Go ahead and smile. We're away from Legate for the day."

A sweet smile curled her lips. "That means nobody's watching."

"Not a soul."

He leaned in for a kiss that went deeper than their usual pecks on the cheek. He ran his fingers through her silky blond hair and—

"Ew! Gross!" Charlie peered into the minivan. "You shouldn't do that to my mom."

Roman growled, "Your mom likes it."

"But I don't." Charlie stomped his feet as he stormed toward Claudette's front door.

"This could be a problem," Anya said. "Charlie's jealous of my attention."

"I'll work it out with him."

"You sound sure of yourself."

Patiently, he explained. "I've managed negotiations with heads of state, with geniuses and pundits and the media."

"But you've never had to deal with a five-year-old before."

"How hard could it be?"

"Oh, you poor naive man." She rolled her eyes. "You have no idea what you're in for."

They followed Charlie into Claudette's charming two-story Victorian. In keeping with the old-fashioned atmosphere, she'd used antiques in her decor. But the character of her house came from the many interesting objects she'd picked up in her travels: Chinese vases, African masks, Nepalese rugs, squat pre-Columbian statues and delicate Venetian blown glass. The photographs hanging on the walls were more varied than those of any travel agency.

Claudette shooed them away from the kitchen. "Go. Keep Charlie occupied. I need to finish cooking."

"Can I help?" Anya asked.

"No, thank you. This is my dinner. It's been years since I made a turkey, and I'm rather enjoying the process." She pirouetted toward the kitchen. "Five minutes."

Shuffling into the front room, Anya muttered, "I don't think she's ever done a whole Thanksgiving dinner."

"Not even when you were a kid?"

She shook her head. "There were only the two of us. So it didn't make much sense. When we attended family events, my mother was always the person who brought some bizarre inedible dish to educate everybody else."

"Such as?"

"I remember something with yams in a goopy yellow sauce that she tried to pass off as the staple diet of the Tsetse tribe."

"A tribe that worships the mosquito?"

"Totally fictional." She grinned. "I guess I did inherit something from my mother, after all. We're both lousy cooks."

Roman gallantly kept his mouth shut.

In the predicted five minutes, they were seated around the table. After a quick grace, Anya silently counted her blessings, starting with Charlie. Her son was healthy and smart and adorable even though he was going through an annoying obstreperous phase. She was also thankful that her mother was healthy and relatively happy. And that left Roman.

She passed the turkey and smiled at him. There was much in their relationship that pleased her. His sense of humor. His strength and his protectiveness. And the sex, of course, was transcendent. She still had a few suspicions, but they were minor.

"Do you like the stuffing?" Claudette asked.

"It's excellent, Mother."

Trying to remain positive, Anya seized on another reason
for thanks: Her mother had chosen to prepare a traditional
dinner. No snails. No fried cockroaches.

It wasn't until Charlie had eaten as much as T-Rex and
the plates were cleared that Claudette revealed her dinner
surprise. "I've invited a couple more people for after-
dinner drinks."

Anya winced. Dread threatened her sunny mood.
"Who?"

"Fredrick and that nice Dr. Neville."

Fredrick Slater was coming here, invading Anya's stolen
moment of contentment. Until now, she'd managed to
avoid any lengthy confrontation with him. She didn't trust
herself to face him without lashing out.

"They couldn't make it for dinner," Claudette said.
"Some other boring commitment. But I wanted them to
have some family time."

Why? Her mother had always given her the impression
that family was the boring part. Her energies focused on
her career.

Anya glanced over at Charlie who had already collapsed
on the sofa. He'd be okay if she slipped away, and she
needed some downtime to regroup before she met Slater.
She went to the coat closet and grabbed her pea jacket.
"I'm going for a walk."

"Great idea," Roman said. "I'll join you."

"Hurry back," Claudette called out.

They were at the door when the chimes rang. Anya's
hand rested on the knob. How could she make small talk
with Slater? He might be responsible for the death of a
village. He might have lit the fuse on the explosion that
killed her husband.

"Be calm," Roman said softly. "I'm right here beside
you."

When the chime sounded again, she yanked the door open. Fredrick Slater and his right-hand man, Dr. Neville, stood on the step. Their smiles were white and bright—like those of a couple of man-eating sharks.

"Come in," she said through her own tightly clenched teeth.

Claudette danced toward them and trilled her greetings, clearly delighted to welcome these very important men into her home.

"Anya and I were just leaving for a walk," Roman said.

"I'll join you," Slater said, patting his stomach. "The exercise will do me good."

"We were planning a long walk," Roman said coolly. "Alone."

Slater clapped him on the shoulder. "Surely you lovebirds can put up with me for a few blocks." He gestured to the door. "Shall we?"

As they strolled along the sidewalk, Roman carefully positioned himself between her and Slater. Anya had to admire Roman's effort to keep the conversation casual and comfortable. He talked about turkey and Thanksgiving and the weather.

Nonetheless, her mood darkened. She hated this man. Slater had taken a renowned think tank and used it for his own evil aims. She couldn't forget, wouldn't forgive.

Not even the charm of Washington Square distracted her. The ornate white spires of Saints Peter and Paul Church reminded her of truth and purity. How could she spend time in the company of a man who had possibly caused the death of her husband?

"This park," Roman said, "was named for George Washington. But the bronze statue is Benjamin Franklin."

"Not exactly fair to Ben," she said.

"Nor to George," Slater said. He gestured toward a wrought-iron bench. "Sit here beside me, Anya."

"I'd rather stand."

"Please." He patted the bench.

Swallowing her antipathy, she perched at the edge of the bench. Roman sat on her other side.

"Charlie's doing very well at school," Slater said. "Don't you agree?"

"Yes," she said tersely.

"But I'm concerned about you, my dear young lady. What can I do to make you happy?"

She turned her head toward him and stared coldly. His sins weren't branded across his face, and some people—including her mother—might think him a handsome older gentleman. Yet Anya saw a sinister cast in the depths of his eyes. A shadow behind the facade. "I'm fine," she said.

"You've made friends with other parents at the school, and you're developing a relationship with Roman." He reached over and rested his long-fingered hand on Anya's knee. "How's your work situation? Tell me about your language class in the city."

Her heart skipped a beat. How much did he know? Legate security might have followed her. They might have seen her father on the street and reported to Slater. "The classes are fine."

"You're studying Bantu?"

"Yes." The language of the people in Topaku, the people who had died from a mysterious virus.

In a very subtle way, Slater was threatening her, and she didn't like it. Anya knew she shouldn't say anything to him, but—

"We should be getting back," Roman said. He must have sensed her hostility and hoped to defuse this potentially explosive situation. "Claudette is waiting."

"Anya," Slater said. "I sense there's something you want to share with me."

She hated the smug expression on his face, the arch of his eyebrow, the sneer of his lips. "As a matter of fact, Fredrick, there is something I'd like to share. I want to get the hell away from Legate."

He smiled indulgently. "What do you mean, my dear? Where do you want to go?"

"Anywhere else. I want to activate the escape clause in our contract."

He leaned forward ever so slightly, encouraging her to continue. "Why?"

Before she could answer, Roman said, "Anya has been feeling homesick for Denver."

"She can go back to Colorado for a visit anytime she wants," Slater said.

"With Charlie," she said.

"That's unacceptable. You can't pull your son out of school. What's this really about, Anya?"

"I don't have to give a reason." Her heart was beating in triple time. Now that she'd started, there was no backing down. "My contract is clear. I pay you back and our relationship is ended."

"Of course." His lips curved in an ominous smile. "Let's see now. Moving expenses and travel costs. You've been here for a couple of months. Your personal expenses include rental for the cottage, food and services."

"Yes," she said. This seemed easy...too easy.

He continued. "In addition to the regular tuition for Charlie's schooling, there would be additional costs for his hours with special instructors—the Nobel laureates and the renowned specialists. Their time, I regret to inform you, is billed at six hundred to a thousand dollars per hour. And Charlie's sessions at the stables."

"How much?"

"If I had to hazard a guess, I'd say we were somewhere in the neighborhood of one million dollars."

Her head was spinning. She had no concept of how much these things would cost. The contract had been too vague. She should have nailed down those numbers. "I don't have anywhere near that much money."

"No, I don't expect you do."

She surged to her feet. "You can't force me to stay here."

"You can go whenever you want," he said. "But I've made a substantial investment in your son's education. Charlie stays with me."

She felt Roman's hand on her arm, holding her back. As if she could make this worse?

Slater rose from the park bench and straightened the lapels of his coat. "I don't care to know what this tantrum is really about. Anya, I suggest you get over yourself. Charlie deserves a mother who will support and encourage his genius. I only hope you're up to the task."

He turned on his heel and walked away from Washington Square without looking back.

A brisk wind coiled around her, strangling her. She'd been a fool to think she could outsmart Slater.

Still standing behind her, Roman embraced her. His arms were strong, steady and reassuring, but she was not comforted.

"Okay," Roman said, "that went well."

"Can Slater do that?" She leaned against his chest. "Can he make up expenses?"

"Unfortunately, he's not lying. Legate charges an incredible fee for consultation with many of our staff." He rested his chin on top of her head. "I should have seen this coming. There were no dollar amounts in your contract.

One of the clever Legate accountants can tabulate a bill for you that's beyond the federal deficit.''

"I need a lawyer," she said.

He leaned close and whispered, "What we need is patience. And truth."

"To put Legate out of business."

"Speak softly, Anya. Assume that we're being overheard."

His warm breath on her ear should have excited her, but she was cold—frozen from the inside out. "How can someone listen?"

"Long-range bugging equipment could be focused on us at this very moment. The best thing is to keep walking, to get in a crowd."

She knew exactly where they had to go. "Chinatown."

Chapter Thirteen

After her disastrous confrontation with Slater, Anya was itching for action. But Roman forced a leisurely pace as they strolled at the edge of Washington Square. She fidgeted impatiently. "Could we hurry, please?"

He leaned close to her ear and whispered, "People are watching and listening."

"I don't care."

Speaking ever so softly, he said, "You tried the direct approach with Slater, and it didn't accomplish much."

She had to agree with him. Blurting out her concerns had been spectacularly unsuccessful.

"Now," Roman said, "we'll do it my way."

She nodded. "Okay."

He stepped back and pointed out a landmark she was already familiar with. "Excellent view of Coit Tower."

What on earth? Was he speaking in code? She glanced dismissively at the lighthouse-shaped structure peeking above the treetops on Telegraph Hill. "It's a little phallic for my taste."

"Did you know," he said, "that it was built with a bequeathment from Lillie Hitchcock Coit to beautify the city? Take a closer look."

Puzzled, she glanced up at his face, seeing only her reflection in his dark Ray-Ban sunglasses. Her lips formed silent words. "What are you trying to tell me?"

"Be observant," he said. "What do you see?"

The park. The benches. The other pedestrians. Beside the statue of Ben Franklin, she saw a short man with a red baseball cap who was taking photos with a huge zoom lens. But his focus was in their direction. There were no landmarks behind them. He was watching them! When he turned away, she was sure of it.

"What do you hear?" Roman asked.

The usual city noises. Snatches of conversation. Traffic sounds. A distant clanging. "Cable car?"

"Let's go."

He grabbed her hand and pulled. In an instant, he'd transformed from idle tourist to a man with a mission. She was hard-pressed to keep up as he ran toward Mason Street.

Roman's timing was perfect. They leaped onto the running board of the cable car as it pulled away from the stop. No one else boarded after them.

With a rattle and a jolt, the cable car chugged toward Chinatown. "Okay," he said. "Now we can talk."

"I need…" She huffed, struggling to catch her breath. "I've got to take a more active part in your investigation. We have to wrap this up. Fast."

He frowned almost pensively. Roman wasn't winded. But, of course, he wouldn't be. He ran at least five miles a day. "It's better if you stay out of it."

"I can't," she said. "I can't just stand around with my thumb up my nose. It makes me nervous. Then I blurt."

"I noticed." He'd wanted to avoid casting suspicion on her, but it was too late. After her demand that Slater let her out of the contract, she'd be watched closely.

"There must be something I can do."

"Continue with the translations I gave you. On memos from Topaku."

"There's nothing in the archived documents." She sank down on the wooden cable car bench. "If real evidence exists, it has to be in the main computer system. It's time to make that search."

"I agree." He sat beside her and draped his arm around her shoulders. Finally, he had some positive news.

Though it wasn't possible for Roman to break through the computer's firewall and search without revealing himself, the CIA could perform that operation. He kissed Anya's cheek. "My contact person is set to break into the Legate computers."

"When?"

"Today. Possibly at this very moment. The search was scheduled for the Thanksgiving holiday when there would be few employees at Legate."

"And they can't suspect you," she said, "because you're here with me. It's a brilliant cover story."

Brilliant? He didn't have one-eighth of her confidence. "As soon as Slater finds out that his computer system has been breached, all hell will break loose. Security at Legate will be ultra-intense."

"But your contact could find proof," she said. "If Legate is guilty of testing that virus at Topaku, this could be over in a matter of hours."

"Don't count on it." He gazed down into her innocent blue eyes. She was much too trusting for undercover work. Deception and manipulation weren't part of her character. "It might be wise for you to take a trip to Colorado."

"And leave Charlie here? By himself?"

"I'd be able to—"

"No," she said. The softness in her eyes turned to steel.

"I know I messed up. I shouldn't have said anything to Slater. It won't happen again."

When the cable car stopped on Jackson, they were two blocks away from Chinatown. "Get off here," Roman said. "We'll be followed again so we need a cover story. Let's go shopping to buy a puzzle box for Charlie."

"Do you think they're listening now?"

"Not yet."

She fell into step beside him. "Who was watching us in the park? Was it the guy in the red baseball cap?"

He nodded. "His camera was probably a listening device."

"It's too bad I can't tell Charlie about all this surveillance stuff. He'd get a kick out of it."

True, there were moments when this game of hide-and-seek was exciting. The thrill of the chase. The secret meetings with Maureen. But Roman was jaded after all these months of being undercover, and he hated always having to watch his back.

They walked downhill into Chinatown. Even on a stay-at-home holiday, the streets were fairly busy.

"By the way," she said. "There's a place here that I want to visit."

He had a good idea of what she was talking about: her father. The last time she was in Chinatown, Wade Bouchard was with her. "Keep your eyes open. Try to see if anybody's following us."

"How could they? We just got here."

Back in the park she'd spoken of Chinatown. The cable car route ended near Chinatown. Any surveillance team worth its salt would figure out their destination. Also, he and Anya would be easy to follow. Roman's height literally made him stand out in a crowd. And Anya's white-blond hair gleamed like a signal flag.

They walked a couple of blocks, then Roman pivoted. They headed back in the direction from which they'd come. He made a quick scan of the other people on the street. Though he was familiar with most of the Legate security staff, these people were pros. They knew how to fade into the scene.

He spotted three possible tails. A well-dressed woman who appeared to be window-shopping. A man with a Raiders cap hiding his features brushed past them. And there was a young guy with headphones that might be listening equipment.

Roman memorized their height and their gait. Even if they changed appearance, he'd know them.

"Double back," he said to Anya.

They turned again, and he waited to see who would follow. The kid with the headphones paused on the street. Signaling for backup?

She grabbed Roman's hand and pulled him into a meat market where no one could see them or aim a listening device at them. "I need to tell you something," she said. "When I came here after my class, I was with someone who—"

"I know," he said. "Wade Bouchard."

"How did you know?"

"CIA surveillance."

"I hate this," she said vehemently. "Everybody is watching everybody else."

"Are you keeping any other secrets?" he asked.

"I should ask you."

The clerk behind the counter called out to them in Chinese, and Anya answered, matching his dialect. They conversed for a moment, and she took Roman's hand. "This way. There's a back door."

"He told you that?"

"I'm a very persuasive person." She grinned. "He said I could use the rest room."

They slipped through the rear door into a narrow corridor that smelled of fresh fish and incense. Anya glanced up at him. "Do you remember the shop where you found me in Chinatown?"

"Wang Ho's," he said. "It's not far from here."

"My father went into a door in the alley beside that building. If we go back that way, we might find him. Or someone who knows where we can find him."

"Why, exactly, are we looking for your father?"

"He had information about Topaku," she said. "And I want to know where he got it."

Maybe it was worth a shot to contact Wade Bouchard. But Roman doubted her father would be happy to see him. Very likely, he considered Roman to be an enemy.

At the end of the corridor, he shoved open a door. They were in an alley between buildings. He tried a door on the opposite side. Locked!

If they returned to the main thoroughfare, they'd be spotted. He pulled down the ladder on a fire escape. "Going up. You first."

As she climbed the black metal ladder, he had a fine view of her cute little butt in snug gray slacks. Roman wished he had more time to admire. But he went up the ladder right after her.

Their shoes were loud on the metal stairs, but there wasn't time to tiptoe. On the third floor, Anya paused. "Now what?"

He assumed this level was apartments with windows that may or may not be locked. Better not to chance walking in on someone. "Take the ladder to the roof."

In a moment, he was beside her on the flat tar-paper rooftop. Fortunately, this building was not of the tiled pagoda style. It looked like the residents took advantage of this space. There were a couple of lawn chairs and discarded beer bottles. In the center of the roof was a brick structure with a door. He tugged on the handle, and it opened. ''Going down?''

''After you.''

As they descended a narrow twisting staircase, he said, ''Too bad you don't have a cap. Your blond hair stands out.''

''What about you?''

''I'm wearing black. I blend.''

''Silly man.'' She paused to give him a smile and a pat on the cheek. ''Every woman on the street gives you an ogle. You stand out like a tuxedo at a rummage sale.''

''You've got that backward. No red-blooded male can look at you without wanting you.''

''Like you?'' she teased. ''Do you want me?''

''Always.'' He pulled her into his arms. Her sweet lips joined with his, and her slender body pressed against him. She felt good and hot and, yes, he did want her. But he pulled away quickly, not allowing himself to savor their kiss. The last thing he needed was to chase through Chinatown in a fully aroused state. Talk about standing out in a crowd. ''Let's go.''

They descended a staircase through the center of the building, down a corridor and onto the street again. Moving quickly, but not so fast that they'd attract notice, they made it to Wang Ho's—the market where he'd found her the last time they were in Chinatown.

She went down the alley and grasped the knob of a small door. It opened at her touch. Roman had a sense that this was too easy. Her father and the other scientists in SCAT were clever enough to evade the CIA. They wouldn't be found by him and Anya...unless they wanted to make contact.

Slowly, he led the way down a hallway that wasn't wide enough for them to walk abreast. This building was well maintained with clean paint on the walls and black lacquered doors.

As they neared the staircase, a tall Asian man appeared from nowhere. His aged skin seemed thin as parchment. Circling his mouth was a wispy goatee. A long black trench coat fell from his thin shoulders. His hands were hidden in the pockets. Holding a gun?

Roman stepped forward. "Chou Liu?"

The Chinese man nodded slowly.

His name had appeared twice. Once on the registration for the car Peter Bunch was riding in, and again on Anya's class schedule. Roman asked, "Where's Wade Bouchard?"

Chou Liu's face remained impassive. "We can't talk here. Up the stairs."

"Are you armed?"

"Are you?"

"No." Roman had considered wearing an ankle holster, but he hadn't expected today to be anything more than Turkey Day. "It's Thanksgiving."

"I know. I had Peking duck." When Chou Liu grinned, creases spread across his face as though his parchment skin had crinkled. "Second floor. Third door to the left."

As he climbed the staircase, Roman wished there were some way to keep Anya out of this confrontation, but it was too late for second thoughts about safety. Tracking down SCAT might be a case of jumping from the frying pan into the fire.

As they approached the apartment door, it opened. Peter Bunch stood waiting. He didn't bother to be subtle with his gun, but he wasn't aiming at them. "Get in here."

Chou Liu closed the door behind them and leaned against it.

Peter said, "You shouldn't have come."

Roman tended to agree. He and Anya were neatly trapped in this apartment. "What's with all the artillery?"

"Precaution." Still holding his handgun, Peter went to the window in the small apartment. The shade was drawn, and he carefully peeked around the edge. "You've been a Legate man for a long time, Roman. How do we know you're not still on their side?"

"I'm not on anybody's side."

"I worked as your assistant for four months," Peter said. "I didn't see any evidence that you were out to get Legate."

"Then you aren't very observant," Roman said.

"Who are you working with? The Feds? A Legate competitor? The CIA?" He turned away from the window. "None of them can be trusted."

"And you?" Roman asked. "Can you be trusted?"

Peter was part of a very paranoid organization. When he came toward them, his gun was leveled at Roman's midsection. "How do I know you haven't led them here?"

"You don't." Roman's stomach muscles clenched. Beside him, Anya gasped.

"What do you want?" Peter demanded.

"Retribution," Roman said. "I want to know who set the explosion at Building Fourteen. I want to know who killed my friend Jeremy Parrish. And I want them to pay for that murder."

Anya piped up, "And I want to see my father."

"Why?" Peter asked.

Roman shot her a glare that should have told her to keep quiet. It had no effect.

Anya stepped forward. "My father told me about the

Topaku epidemic. Why is he so certain about what happened there?''

''Because we know,'' Peter said.

He lowered his gun, walked two paces and flung his skinny frame into a chair. He dragged a trembling hand through his dirty brown hair. This young man was definitely sailing on the edge in a high wind. He looked like he might capsize at any minute.

''We need more than your suspicions.'' Roman glanced over his shoulder at Chou Liu. ''We need proof about the epidemic.''

''It's all damned obvious.'' Nervously, Peter toyed with the Glock automatic. ''How did the virus get to Topaku if not through Legate?''

''There are ways,'' Roman said. Carefully, he moved to include Chou Liu in the conversation. Roman had a feeling that the impassive Chinese man represented the real power in SCAT. ''Let's talk basic epidemiology. Virus usually spreads through animals. The livestock at Topaku were infected. Who knows how they caught it?''

''There's one person who knew,'' Peter said. ''A scientist who was familiar with the village.''

''His name was Aringa,'' Anya said. ''He occasionally worked for Legate, and he was in the village. I read his notes from the archives, and he said nothing about the virus being purposely released.''

''Then you didn't read the right notes,'' Peter snapped. He glanced toward the door. ''It's best if you both leave. I don't want anybody else to find us.''

Anya planted her feet. ''I'm not going anywhere until I talk to my father.''

Roman was fairly sure that taking a stand wasn't the smartest approach. Anya had the worst undercover technique he'd ever seen. She acted like Joan of Arc, charging into battle on a white stallion. Very noble. Very likely to be burned at the stake.

"What she means," he said, "is how can we contact Wade Bouchard?"

"He will contact you," Chou Liu said.

Roman confronted him directly. "And you? How can I reach you?"

"I sometimes get messages through the language school."

Roman nodded. "And how do you believe the virus was spread."

"Through the water supply," he said. "One well served the village. One well infected animals and humans alike."

His theory made sense, except for one thing. "But the villagers got sick at different times."

"Incubation period varies based on metabolism, antibodies and natural immunities." He spoke with the calm authority of a scientist. "It is likely that the water supply was poisoned with the virus."

"By Legate," Roman said. For the first time, he actually believed all these allegations about the Topaku epidemic. Of all the heinous things Legate had done, this was by far the worst. Experimentation on human beings—innocent men, women and children. "They poisoned the water."

"One well," Chou Liu repeated.

"How do we find proof?"

"A water sample was taken by Aringa. Find it." When he turned to Anya, his lips smiled within the circle of his goatee. "Your father wishes the best for you and your son."

"How can I find him?" she asked. "I need his help to get away from Legate."

"Come to Chinatown for the Chinese New Year celebration."

"That's months from now." Her voice betrayed her disappointment. "I can't wait that long."

"Bring the boy. We will help you escape." Chou Liu opened the apartment door. "Now you must go."

Roman whisked her into the hallway before she could raise another objection. Working undercover with her was like carrying a live grenade in his pocket.

"I can't wait two months," she said. "I'll go crazy."

And she would probably take him along into crazy land with her. He herded her down the staircase. "Before we go out on the street, I need a promise from you, Anya. Please don't arrange meetings with anyone without informing me."

"Not even with my own father?"

"Especially not with him." He stared deep into her eyes. "This is dangerous territory. You saw the guns. You heard what Chou Liu said. If Legate killed all those people, Slater will be desperate to cover up. He might lash out."

But Roman saw no evidence of fear in her expression. Her sharp little chin thrust forward. Her eyes were clear. "I promise to be careful."

As he stepped into the sunlight on the street, he turned on the cell phone. There were four messages from Slater. Roman had a feeling that the spit had just hit the fan.

He punched in the speed dial for Slater's cell phone. "Yes, sir."

"Where the hell are you?"

"Anya and I went to Chinatown, looking for a puzzle box for Charlie." He glanced at the pugnacious woman walking beside him. "I think she's calmed down, sir."

"We have a bigger problem than Anya's ridiculous little snit," Slater said. "A security breach at Legate. Someone broke into our main computer system. When I find out who's responsible for this, heads will roll."

FREDRICK SLATER CLOSED the door to his office. He needed a moment alone. The tasteful elegance of his surroundings failed to soothe his blinding rage. Someone dared encroachment, dared to threaten him. His impregnable computer security had been penetrated. A massive download had taken place. The hounds were on his trail.

He strode to his desk. They wouldn't stop him. No one could stop him. The Legate Corporation was a powerful empire with international influence. His empire.

This intrusion was a nuisance. Nothing more.

His gaze focused on the Degas painting. Behind it was his wall safe. He should destroy the Topaku samples, lose them in the biohazard disposal system.

But he had a better idea.

Chapter Fourteen

Back at Anya's cottage on the Legate grounds, it was clear to her that Charlie was the only person who had enjoyed Turkey Day. He had a new puzzle box that he'd solved, refitted and solved again. And his tummy was stuffed with good food.

Anya left her mother in the living room as she took Charlie upstairs and helped him get ready for bed.

"Mommy, I ate a lot."

"You did, indeed." She tidied up his room, which was a little larger than her own. Charlie needed extra space for his eclectic combination of toys and high-tech computer equipment.

"Mr. Slater was in a bad mood."

Mr. Slater was a bad man. "Yes, he was."

The last thing Charlie did before hopping into bed was to set the little dragon from the first puzzle box Roman had given him on the nightstand. He snuggled under the covers and looked up at her. "Why was he angry? Did I do something wrong?"

"Absolutely not. Sometimes grown-ups, like Mr. Slater, get upset about grown-up things. And it doesn't have anything to do with you." She sat on the bed and hugged him close. His small body felt fragile in her arms. "I love you, sweetpea."

"I love you back, Mommy." He wriggled free. "Does Mr. Slater love me?"

"I'm sure he does."

"And Grandma?"

"Definitely."

"And Roman?"

"You bet," she said. "Roman loves you a whole bunch."

"I think he loves you," Charlie said as he flung himself back on the pillows. "Do you love Roman?"

She hesitated. Charlie's question was simple and deserved a simple response. But she knew better than to underestimate her son's intuitive reasoning ability. "There are all kinds of love, sweetpea. Roman is a good friend who cared very much about your daddy."

"You loved Daddy," Charlie said with assurance.

"In a special way." She kissed his forehead and pulled up the covers. "The important thing to remember is that you, Charlie, are loved by many people."

"And I can eat more than anybody." He closed his eyes.

After she turned on his dinosaur night-light, she closed her son's bedroom door and went downstairs where her mother was waiting. Anya didn't expect to find a whole bunch of love in the impending conversation with Claudette, who had insisted on coming home with her because they had to talk.

Her mother had brewed a cup of herbal tea. She sat at the kitchen table with her legs neatly crossed. Not a hair was out of place.

"How could you?" she asked.

Anya sat opposite her. "I assume you're referring to my conversation with Slater."

"He's done so much for Charlie. How could you even think about leaving Legate?"

Anya didn't want to lie, but a strict statement of truth wasn't an option. She couldn't announce her well-founded suspicions about Legate. She might be overheard. And Claudette wouldn't understand.

But there was a different version of truth. Emotional truth. "This is about me," Anya said. "I feel isolated here. I don't really have a life."

"Oh, please." Claudette tapped on the oak tabletop with a manicured fingernail. "Your financial needs are taken care of. You have a job utilizing your translating skills. And it certainly seems like you have a relationship with Roman. What else could you possibly want?"

Anya rested her elbows on the table and gazed directly into her mother's eyes. "My restlessness is your fault, Mother."

"Me? Whatever do you mean?"

"Think about the way you raised me. We lived all over the world. We went from one exciting place to another. How can you expect me to settle down forever on these few secluded acres?"

Claudette's thin lips pursed. "I never considered that perspective."

"You led an exotic life, Mother. Why shouldn't I?"

There was a shimmer at the edge of Claudette's perfectly made-up eyes. The hint of a tear? "I never thought I was much good as a mother. Do you think of me as a role model?"

A role model? Her mother was hypercritical, demanding and selfish. But she was also strong, intelligent and well respected. Claudette kicked butt. She never backed down to anyone. Quietly, Anya said, "I wouldn't mind a whole lot if I turned out like you."

Claudette reached across the table, and Anya clasped her hand. The skin felt dry as a wilted flower. This was an odd moment. Her mother had never been big on physical displays of affection.

"We're not so different," Claudette said. "Both single mothers, trying to do the best for our children and still engage in a worthwhile life."

"Happy Thanksgiving, Mother."

"Don't you worry." Claudette pulled her hand back. "We'll find a way for you to have the exciting life you want and still provide Charlie with a Legate education."

Though Anya knew that plan was impossible, she nodded. "Everything is going to be all right."

The special moment faded when Anya heard a knock at the door. Roman stepped inside. He glanced between them. "Am I interrupting?"

"Certainly not." Claudette finished her tea and stood. "I'm awfully tired, Anya. Would you mind if I spent the night?"

"Not at all."

As Claudette passed behind her, she gave Roman a little shove toward her daughter. "You might want to spend the night, as well."

Anya rolled her eyes. "That's very subtle, Mother."

"Just a suggestion." She paused at the staircase and smiled her blessing on both of them. "Like mother, like daughter."

As Claudette vanished up the staircase, Roman approached. "What was that about?"

"Girl talk."

A perplexed smile curled his lips. "Did I just hear your mother say that I should spend the night?"

"I'd rather go to your place."

As they left the cottage, she noticed Harrison, the security guard, talking to someone. It took Anya a moment to recognize Jane Coopersmith away from her receptionist desk. Though she hoped their conversation was nothing more than a friendly chat, she suspected that this was another way to intrude on her privacy.

Jane remembered everything.

IN THE CAR, Roman filled her in on the situation at Legate. "Basically, it boils down to two things—the main computer security failed, resulting in a massive download. And Slater is furious."

"What a shame!" Her voice was sarcastic. "Do they know who did the download?"

"Not yet," Roman said. "Tomorrow morning, a gang of Legate attorneys will converge. Lawsuits will fly in all directions. Slater sounded like he intended to have the computer security reconfigured by Bill Gates himself."

"So my demand to get out of the contract is likely to go unnoticed."

"Not completely," Roman said. In a moment of relative calm, Slater had ordered him to find out what was wrong with her. "But Slater doesn't suspect anything more than moodiness on your part."

"I guess there are certain advantages to not being taken seriously."

"I think he referred to you as the skinny blond broad."

"A skinny broad." She shrugged. "Isn't that an oxymoron?"

Roman hadn't expected to find her in such a good mood. Usually, when Anya spent time with Claudette, she was cranky. "Had a good talk with your mother?"

"Surprisingly good," she said. "We might even have a few things in common. It was nice. I feel like we're really a family."

When he pulled into his garage, Roman immediately noticed the blinking blue light on his security system. It should have been solid red. "Don't start singing the theme song for *Happy Days* just yet."

As the garage door closed behind him, he reached into his glove compartment and took out his 9mm Smith & Wesson, a neat little automatic that fired eleven rounds. "Someone's in my house."

"Shouldn't the alarm be going off?"

"They must have done an override on the system."

"Who do you think it is?"

There were too many possibilities. Legate security. Someone from SCAT. "Damned if I know."

"What should I do?" she asked.

He couldn't allow her to walk into certain danger. "Stay here in the car. If I don't come out in five minutes, back out of here fast and call the police."

"Are you saying I should back out through the closed garage door?"

"That's right." The intruder wouldn't expect that. "Element of surprise. It might be the only way you can escape."

Before she could object, he stepped out of the car and strode to the door leading into his kitchen. Holding his gun at the ready, Roman turned on the kitchen lights. He saw no one.

Had the intruder already left? Quickly, he scanned the open space of the living room. Nothing seemed out of place.

Slowly, Roman looked up toward the ceiling. The intruder had to be in his bedroom. Damn! There was no way to climb the stairs without being vulnerable. Roman had planned it that way. His bedroom was his fortress.

When he stepped onto the stairs, he heard a voice. "It's me. Maureen."

He charged up the stairs and saw his red-haired CIA contact lounging comfortably on the sofa with a drink in her hand. Maureen grinned. "Quite a place you've got here."

"What are you doing here? Why did you—"

"Did you bring your friend with you?"

Anya! Any second she'd be crashing through his garage door and calling the cops.

Roman dashed down the stairs to the garage. Anya was behind the steering wheel with the engine revved and ready to roll.

"False alarm," he yelled, waving his arms.

She stepped out of the car. "Too bad. I was looking forward to playing demolition derby with your Mercedes."

"Why am I not surprised?" She might look like an angel, but she'd proved her devilish tendencies more than once. He grabbed her hand and pulled her through the house. "There's somebody I want you to meet."

Roman went first into the bedroom. "Computer on."

"Welcome home, Roman," said the computer. "It's 10:17."

"Computer, music." He pointed Anya toward the red-haired beauty on the sofa. "This is my CIA contact, Maureen."

He went directly toward the wet bar. After a day like this, he wanted something stronger than wine. "Drinks, ladies?"

"I have one," Maureen said as she stood and extended her hand. "I'm pleased to finally meet you, Anya."

"Thank you." Anya eyed the CIA woman with a combination of suspicion and envy. Maureen was fabulous. Her thick red hair cascaded past her shoulders. She was dressed all in black—tight jeans and a snug T-shirt. Her body was to die for. "How long have you and Roman been in contact?"

"Almost a year." Her handshake was firm. "I was the third person assigned to him. Our cover was that we were dating."

"Makes sense. Given Roman's reputation as a ladies' man." Mentally, Anya calculated the odds that Roman had been sleeping with this gorgeous spy. Very likely. "So you must be familiar with the house."

"Actually, this is the first time I've been inside the fabled den of seduction." Maureen met her gaze with a forthright directness that defused Anya's jealousy. "My relationship with Roman is strictly business."

"Not true," Roman said as he rejoined them. "She's a mother hen who doesn't hesitate to give personal advice."

"Only when you're being an ass." Maureen grinned at Anya. "That's happened a lot less often since he's been with you."

"What do you mean?"

"Okay, one personal comment. Then I'm moving on to business." Maureen glanced from one to the other. "My job is observation. Lately, I've been focused on the two of you. You're a perfect example of how opposites attract."

"Go on," Anya said.

"He's dark. You're light. He's intense and brooding. You're as open as sunshine. Everything he lacks, you have. And vice versa." She shrugged. "You're the perfect match. When this is all over, I fully expect to be invited to the wedding."

"Wedding?" Anya's voice squeaked. She hadn't thought that far ahead. To get married again? To Roman? The very idea was overwhelming. She wasn't ready for marriage.

"Anya, can I get you a drink?" Roman asked.

"I'll have what you're having."

"Whiskey neat?"

"Bring it on."

Maureen checked her wristwatch. "I need to brief you on the computer break-in at Legate."

When Roman returned with her drink, Anya sat on the sofa and listened. But her mind was preoccupied with Maureen's assessment of her relationship with Roman. It was hard to imagine a man like him—a man of action and power—settling down to the sort of secure, quiet home life she envisioned for Charlie and herself.

"In short," Maureen concluded after a detailed explanation of computer software and hardware, "the download was successful in terms of information gathered."

"The codes I provided..." Roman said. "Is there any way they can be traced back to me?"

"Negative. We used your information only as backup to make sure we were on the right track. You are not implicated."

"What did you get?" he asked.

"We captured an incredible volume of data, spanning the last ten years."

"Medical records?" he asked.

"Everything," she said.

This sounded like good news to Anya. If the CIA possessed evidence that Legate had done wrong, charges would be brought. Somehow she doubted it would be that simple. "What's the downside?"

"It's going to take a while to process all this information," Maureen said.

"How long?"

"Days. Maybe weeks."

Frustrated, Anya glanced at Roman, who was sitting beside her on the sofa. Then she looked back at Maureen.

"How can it be that difficult? You're looking for one thing—specific information on the Topaku epidemic."

"Anya's right," Roman said.

Maureen shifted in the chair beside the sofa. She crossed her long legs. "You have no idea how complicated an investigation of this nature can be."

"The hell I don't," Roman said.

"All you need," Anya said, "is the memo from an African biochemist named Aringa. It's possibly written in Bantu."

"The alleged memo," Maureen corrected her.

"Can't you do a computer scan?" Anya fought to keep the pleading tone from her voice. "How many Bantu memos can there be?"

"Even if we find the memo, this scientist is deceased," Maureen pointed out.

"So?"

"We can't use him as a witness, and we're not going to move against Legate until we have an airtight case."

Roman drained the whiskey in his glass. "So, you're telling us to be patient."

"That's why I came here in person," she said. "I need to ask you both to maintain the status quo. Keep a low profile. Make no major changes in your habits. Not until we're ready to move against Legate."

"I don't like this deal," Roman growled.

"You, of all people, should understand," Maureen said. "Fredrick Slater is a well-connected, powerful man. It's going to take a lot to bring him down."

"He's a murderer," Anya said with more vehemence than she intended.

Maureen stood. "We'll get Slater. But it's going to take time. Do you understand?"

Slowly, Anya nodded. How on earth would she find the

fortitude to stay at Legate for weeks or months? "I won't wait forever. The well-being of my child is at stake."

The look Maureen gave her was pure empathy. "This must be hell for you. I'm so sorry."

Sorry didn't make it better. "If there's the slightest hint of danger—"

"Agreed," Maureen said quickly. "We'll get you out of Legate and put you into a federal protection program."

Oh, swell. Another form of confinement. "I'd rather avoid that option."

"For now, I guarantee there's no threat. Slater values the boy's intellect. He'd never hurt Charlie."

How could she be so sure? Apprehension tightened inside Anya, tying her stomach in a knot. She felt certain that Maureen knew something. There was a secret connected to Charlie. "Why do you say that?"

The tall, red-haired woman strode toward the staircase. "Promise me you'll be patient."

"I'll only wait until Chinese New Year," Anya said. Then she would take the escape option offered by her Chou Liu.

"Sounds fair to me," Roman said.

Maureen nodded. "I'll be in touch."

"By the way," Roman said, "how the hell did you get past my house security system?"

"You don't really want to know." She started down the stairs. "I'll reactivate the system on my way out."

Roman watched her depart and leaned back on the sofa, slipping his arm around Anya's shoulders. "Are you okay?"

She tilted back her head to look up at him. "It's a lot to think about."

He didn't want her to ponder too deeply. Maureen had almost slipped up and told her about Slater's plans for

Charlie. If Roman had his way, that information would never come to light.

"I like Maureen," she said, "in spite of the fact that she's gorgeous."

"Is she? I hadn't noticed."

"Yeah, right." She grinned. "I'll bet you can tell me her height, weight and cup size."

He didn't deny it. "So, what did you think about Maureen's theory that opposites attract?"

"We're opposites," Anya said. "That's true."

"And the attraction?"

She glided her hand along his cheek. "I don't find you totally repulsive."

He brushed her lips with a light kiss. "You're not too grotesque yourself."

"In fact," she said as she moved around to position herself on his lap, "you have certain features that I like very much."

"Such as?"

She reached up past his forehead and twisted her fingers in his hair. "This mop. So black and shiny. Like a Labrador retriever."

Her wiggling around on his lap was having the predictable effect. The tension and stress of the day began to fade.

"Here's what I like," he said as he cupped her perfectly round breasts.

"They're not as big as Maureen's," she said.

"Just right for me." He gazed into her wide, blue eyes. "Should we be talking about anything serious?"

"I'd rather not talk," she said suggestively. "You're a man of action."

"You bet." That was all he needed to hear. Holding her in his arms, he stood and carried her to his bed.

Chapter Fifteen

The next three weeks crept by slower than a three-toed sloth. With no word or solid evidence from the CIA, Anya's tension hiked day by day. She found herself visiting Roman as much as possible; the only place she felt secure was in his bedroom. There, they could talk without fear of being overheard. They found time for laughter. And they made love. Oh, did they make love!

On a Wednesday, she arrived at his house just before nine o'clock in the morning while Charlie was in school. Using her key, she opened his front door and expertly plugged in the code to disarm and reactivate the alarm. "Roman? Where are you?"

"Here," he called out.

She strode confidently through the ultramodern decor that had once been intimidating but now felt more like home than her cosy cottage. She found him outside on the deck.

Wearing only his short black robe, he gazed down at the dramatic seascape where the dark bay waters churned and eddied against the cliffside. He came out here often to absorb the view. Sometimes he stood with his shoulders back, looking like the master of all he surveyed. Other times he leaned pensively against the railing, finding solace in the rhythm of the waves.

During these past weeks, she had learned to read the nuance of his moods. Right now, she could tell by the set of his shoulders that he had bad news. The fact that he didn't turn to greet her spoke volumes.

"I thought you'd be dressed," she said. "Remember? We had plans to do Christmas shopping."

He nodded as if he hadn't quite heard her.

She craned her neck to see his face. The wind swept through his thick black hair, brushing it back from his forehead. His cheeks were reddened by the cold and she wondered how long he had been standing here. "What's wrong?"

"We'll go inside to talk."

Though his insistence that they might be observed or overheard in the downstairs portion of his home seemed overly cautious, she didn't object.

In his bedroom, he announced, "I finally heard from Maureen."

Anya braced herself. "What did she say?"

"The CIA has given up. After searching through the computer data, they can't find proof that Legate was responsible for the epidemic in Topaku."

"What about the memo written in Bantu?"

At the wet bar, he poured himself a cup of coffee. "There's nothing."

Disappointment stabbed through her. Her best hopes had been invested in the CIA finding proof. All other leads had evaporated. Though she'd gone into San Francisco to attend a couple of classes at the Institute of International Languages, she hadn't been contacted by her father or Chou Liu.

Anya was keenly aware that every day she spent at

Legate added to the already impossible monetary debt she owed Slater. "This can't be right," she said. "There has to be proof."

"That's what I thought," Roman said. "So did the CIA. That's why they took the risk of breaking into the Legate computer system."

"Slater must have destroyed the memo."

"Either that or it was sent to a computer not connected to the Legate system."

"What do you mean?"

"An e-mail," he said. "The African biochemist, Aringa, might have sent a message to one of the other scientists on their private home computer."

"Can't the CIA search those computers?"

"It's more complicated than simply tapping in," he said. "The memo has probably been erased. Which means we'd have to take the computers so we could scan the hard drives. No way will these guys voluntarily hand over their laptops."

"Jeremy had a laptop," she said.

"I remember." A smile touched the corner of Roman's mouth. "Hardly used the damn thing. He preferred to work in longhand."

"No," she said. "He used it all the time."

Her mind flashed on the memory of Jeremy hunched over his computer late one night, typing with two fingers. Lost in research, he didn't notice her entering the room. When she turned on the overhead light, he swiveled in his desk chair. Behind his wire-frame glasses, his eyes were startled, as though he'd been awakened from a deep sleep.

Then he laughed and beckoned to her. No matter how dedicated Jeremy was to his work, he always made time for her and for Charlie.

Thinking of him had become less painful. Sometimes she

imagined that he was close to her, standing right behind
her. She could almost see the sweet smile on his face. He
would have approved of her relationship with Roman. Jeremy wanted her to be happy. To have fun.

"Even if Jeremy had received the memo in the form of
an e-mail," Roman said, "his computer was destroyed."

"No, it wasn't," she said. "I remember packing it up
when I cleared out his office."

"Are you sure?"

"Totally sure." Though her husband was a scientific
man, he didn't trust computer systems. "He backed up all
his research, especially the work he did at Legate, by sending himself e-mails on the computer at our house. He told
me it was like making a duplicate copy so nothing would
get lost."

"Where is this computer?"

"In storage with the rest of my stuff."

"You're brilliant."

He dragged her into his arms and kissed her hard on the
lips. A familiar and totally wonderful surge of energy jolted
through her. Though their lovemaking had taken on a familiar cadence, like the countdown to a rocket launch, the
blastoff was endlessly exciting.

Roman broke away from her and said, "We need to go
there. To storage."

Without further explanation, he strode across the bedroom and went into the adjoining bathroom.

For a moment, she stood and stared at the closed bathroom door. Her lips were tingling. Her mind was confused.
Why was she brilliant?

Anya went to the bathroom door and eased it open.
When she heard water running in the shower, she went
inside. Roman stood inside the glass stall with three water

jets rinsing his body. His amazing body. Neatly muscled chest. Lean torso. Tight butt.

Staring at him, she almost forgot why she'd come in here. Then she found her voice. "Roman, I don't understand."

"The memo," he said over the gush of the water jets. "It might be on Jeremy's computer."

"But he wasn't working on the Topaku project."

"Jeremy was a biochemist. Just like the African scientist Aringa."

She still wasn't convinced. Jeremy was amazingly intelligent but not an expert in languages. He couldn't even order in a French restaurant. "Why would anyone send him a memo written in Bantu?"

From the shower, Roman said, "What happened when he got foreign e-mail?"

"He asked me to translate." She searched her memory. Vaguely, she recalled a mention of a translation in African dialect. She'd been busy with…something or another. She glanced at the e-mail and said it was too hard. *She had actually seen the memo.* "It was there all the time. Right under my nose."

The irony was almost too much. She'd allowed the proof to slip through her fingers. What a price she'd paid! Especially during these past few weeks when she'd developed a crick in her neck from constantly looking over her shoulder. "Why didn't I remember? It's so obvious."

"Right," he said. "I should have figured it out."

Roman peered through the glass shower toward her. For a moment, he considered the very pleasant idea of hauling her in here with him and peeling off her clothes until she was naked and slick.

He ducked his head under the spray for a final rinse.

There would be plenty of time for him and Anya later. He turned off the water and opened the shower door.

Anya stood in his path, confronting him. "I can't believe I did all this skulking around for nothing!"

"Could you hand me a towel?"

She flung a washcloth at his head. "Do you have any idea how hard these past weeks have been?"

"It wasn't all bad," he said. They'd made love dozens of times. Surely that counted on the plus side.

"It's been easy for you," she said. "You don't have to live at Legate under constant surveillance. I've been a wreck."

Roman grabbed a towel from the rack. "Let's look on the positive side. Maybe Jeremy's computer is the answer."

"Why didn't you mention his laptop before?"

Because he was certain the laptop had been destroyed in the explosion at Building Fourteen. The last time he saw his friend, Roman teased him about not using the computer that sat on the desk at his elbow.

Those poignant final moments came back in vivid detail. He remembered the photograph of Charlie and Anya on the desk. The exhaustion in Jeremy's eyes. His cough. The relief in his voice when he decided to return to his family. Roman tried not to relive that scene. It hurt too much.

He headed toward the door to the bedroom. "I'll be dressed in a minute, and we'll go to the storage unit."

If Jeremy's computer held the proof that would bring down Legate, sweet justice would be served. Via his computer, Jeremy would reach back from the grave to point a damning finger at his murderers.

He dressed quickly and headed toward the staircase. But Anya remained where she was—perched on the edge of his bed with her ankles crossed. Hesitantly, she said, "Maybe we should contact Maureen and let the CIA take care of this.''

Not a chance. Roman was sick and tired of stepping back, leaving the action to someone else. ''It's my turn now.''

As he drove toward the storage area on the outskirts of Oakland, he watched carefully in the rearview mirror. Heavy fog obscured his vision. Though he backtracked and took side roads, he couldn't be one hundred percent sure no one was following them.

''What happens if we find the memo?'' Anya asked.

''That depends on what the memo says. How are your translating skills in Bantu?''

''Not too shabby,'' she said.

Making a sharp right turn, he drove to the main gate for Seashore Storage. No one else was there. The security at this unmanned facility was minimal, nothing more than a chain-link fence and a couple of video cameras. Anya used her key to open the main gate, and they drove slowly on a narrow asphalt road that ran through the metal sheds to her garage-size unit.

Before getting out of the Mercedes, Roman took his handgun from the glove compartment and fastened the holster to his belt.

''Is that necessary?'' she asked.

''Better safe than sorry.''

With a shrug, she approached the unit. ''It might take a while. There's a lot of stuff in here.''

When she unlocked the sliding door and pulled it up, a mass of cardboard boxes and furniture confronted them. The space looked more tangled than one of Charlie's puzzle boxes.

They started at the left, pulling out cardboard boxes. Roman used his pocket knife to slice through the tape. "These aren't even labeled," he muttered.

"My mother supervised the movers," Anya said. "I'm sure she would have preferred throwing everything out."

"But you remember packing up the laptop."

"I couldn't stand the idea of anybody else touching the things on Jeremy's desk. Toys that Charlie gave him on Father's Day. Photos." There was a catch in her voice. "I guess that's why I packed up a perfectly good laptop instead of using it. There were too many memories attached."

He watched as she made her way deeper into the unit. She'd already taken off her gloves, and she made a quick swipe at the corner of her eye. Dashing away a tear? This search had to be difficult for her. When Jeremy died, Roman had lost a friend. But Anya had lost her life mate. "If you want to wait in the car, I can dig through here on my own."

"It's okay." She pulled out a box that seemed lightweight. "I've been planning to come here anyway. I wanted to find the box with Christmas decorations. Try this one."

He sliced open the lid. "Stuffed animals."

"Close it. Charlie already has his favorites."

For half an hour, they sorted through boxes. Several contained papers from Jeremy's file cabinets, which they decided to load into the trunk and search through later.

"Here it is," Anya said. She pointed to an oddly shaped flat box. "The laptop is in there."

Roman placed the box in the back seat. "We're done."

"Not quite yet." She climbed over an ottoman and leaned around a bookshelf, disappearing into the rear of the storage unit. She emerged with a carton containing a fake Christmas tree. "And there's at least one more box with ornaments."

As she burrowed back into the unit, he smiled. The contrasting goals of their search amused him. A laptop computer that might hold incredible secrets. And Christmas ornaments. This had to be the all-time strangest combination of espionage and domesticity.

It turned out that there were two more boxes with decorations. Roman crammed them into the back seat and trunk. "Is that everything?"

"We should have brought the minivan," she said.

Before he could slam the trunk lid, he heard the whisper of tire treads against asphalt. Another vehicle had pulled up behind his Mercedes.

Peter Bunch leaped from the driver's seat. As he approached, he aimed his handgun. "What have we got here?"

"Christmas decorations," Anya said.

"What else?"

He was cold and businesslike, lacking the nervousness he displayed in Chinatown. His gloved hand held the pistol steady.

Roman stepped forward. "This doesn't concern you."

"You found something important," Peter said. "The memo?"

"You're making a mistake." Roman didn't want to draw his gun. Not with Anya standing in the line of fire. He nodded to her. "Get in the car."

"Not so fast." Peter raised his gun arm.

"I don't understand," she said. "I thought you worked for my father."

"Do I?"

"Of course." But her voice was doubtful.

Quietly boastful, he said, "I outsmarted you all."

In an instant, Roman perceived the truth. Though Peter

Bunch had insinuated himself into SCAT, his loyalties lay elsewhere. "You work for Legate."

"Good guess."

"Slater hired you as my assistant," Roman said. "Were you supposed to keep an eye on my activities?"

"You've been under suspicion for a long time," Peter said. "Slater knew there was a leak. Neville figured it was you."

Roman should have known. He should have guessed. "Then you joined up with SCAT. You double-crossed them."

"Enough talk," Peter said. "Do what I say, and nobody gets hurt."

Roman's blood boiled through his veins. He hadn't come this close to finding proof only to hand it over. "Anya, get in the car."

"No," Peter snapped. "She stays here where I can keep an eye on her. I want both of you to load those boxes into my car. Now."

"Fine," Anya said.

When she turned her back on Peter to lift a box from the trunk, she gave Roman a wink. What was she planning? Damn it, he didn't want her involved. She could be hurt. She could be killed. "No," he whispered.

But she carried the box toward Peter, chattering all the way. "You're totally wasting your time. These are my personal things. I have a life, you know. A life that doesn' have anything to do with global intrigue and spying."

She set the box down near Peter's feet. His gun aimed directly at her head, and Roman guessed at the dangerous ploy she was attempting. She meant to distract Peter's attention so Roman could strike.

He wouldn't have done it this way.

She flipped open the lid of the box. "See. Christmas ornaments."

Roman edged closer. He was less than five feet away from Peter Bunch.

She lifted out a wrapped glass ball and tore off the paper. "I got this one for Charlie's first Christmas."

"Just put the damn box in my car," Peter said.

She lifted the star that went at the top of the tree. With a flick of her wrist, she threw the jagged decoration in Peter's face. He raised both hands to protect himself.

Roman charged. There was no time for subtlety. He launched himself at Peter, crashing into him, knocking him to the asphalt. With a quick chop to the wrist, Roman disarmed the other man.

They were both on their feet, circling each other. Peter drew back his fist for a wild roundhouse right, and Roman stepped in for a quick, efficient jab. His fist connected with Peter's jaw.

Though pain shot through Roman's hand and up his arm, the punch felt very, very satisfying. As Peter staggered back, Roman unholstered his gun. "Don't move."

"You won't shoot me." Peter leaned against the fender of his car. Blood trickled from the corner of his mouth, and Roman hoped he'd knocked out a tooth.

Peter pushed himself away from the car. He stood for a moment, weaving on his feet. "I'm leaving."

When he took a step forward, Roman aimed a bullet at the asphalt near the car door. Unfortunately, his marksmanship was rusty. He hit Peter's shoe.

The young man screamed.

Another shot rang out. Peter gasped and clutched at his shoulder.

Roman heard a yell. "CIA. Freeze."

Maureen stepped around the corner of a storage shed.

With her were two marksmen—one with a long-range rifle and the other holding a handgun.

She marched up to Roman, hips swinging like a metronome. In a calm voice, she said, "This is why we like to run operations. When people like you and Anya get involved, things get messy."

"But things get done," Roman said. In one admittedly messy operation, he and Anya had flushed out Peter Bunch, who was spying for Legate. And they'd found Jeremy's computer. "Why were you following us?"

"We weren't. We had a stakeout on him." She nodded toward Bunch, who was being forcibly escorted toward a sleek black vehicle. "I didn't know he was such a prize. Working for Legate while infiltrating SCAT? He'll make a fine source of information."

When Maureen turned toward Anya, her manner changed. Her voice was gentle and soft. "Anya, are you all right?"

"Just dandy." Her hands were shoved in her pockets, and Roman guessed she was hiding the trembling that came in the aftermath of violence.

"You did well," Maureen said. "Throwing the star in his face was quick thinking."

"Maybe I have a talent for this kind of work."

"Let's hope not," Roman said.

Maureen glanced from one to the other. "Why did you come here? What were you looking for?"

Quickly, Roman said, "Christmas decorations."

"And what else?"

"Jeremy's private papers from his files."

"We can take them," Maureen said.

"Hold on," Anya said. "I don't like the idea of strangers pawing through my husband's things. There might be personal notes."

''I understand,'' Maureen said softly. ''I lost someone, too. Someone I loved.''

To Roman's amazement, the two women hugged. He never would have expected that kind of warmth from hard-boiled Maureen. He'd known her for nearly a year and she'd never mentioned her personal tragedy.

With Anya, the CIA agent was different. The two women shared a bond. Women who grieved. Women who wept. Women who mourned the loss of loved ones.

They were softer than men. Yet their strength and endurance were beyond his comprehension. He admired the female spirit. All women seemed precious to him.

Chapter Sixteen

Back at Roman's house, safe in his bedroom, Anya collapsed across the bed. Though it was still before noon, she felt like she'd been through an incredibly long and arduous day.

On the coffee table across the room, Roman opened the box containing Jeremy's personal things and found the laptop computer. "I'll store this in my safe," he said. "Do you know the password to get into Jeremy's files?"

"It's Charlie," she said.

"Tonight after work, I'll start digging."

"After work?" She couldn't believe what she was hearing. Surely he didn't intend to stroll into Legate with his silk necktie knotted around his throat like a noose.

"I have a full schedule this afternoon."

"You can't go in there." She bolted upright on the bed. "You heard what Peter Bunch said. They suspect you."

"All the more reason to show up."

The fear she'd held at bay swept over her like a tidal wave. Earlier, she hadn't been frightened. Not when Peter Bunch waved a gun at them. Not when he was shot by a CIA marksman. In action, there wasn't time to be scared. But now?

The thought of losing Roman terrified her.

She forced herself to take a gulp of air. Her words spilled out in a torrent. "Here's what's going to happen. I'll run home and grab Charlie. We'll all jump in my minivan and we'll run. We'll go fast and far. Nobody will catch us."

He sat beside her on the bed. Gently, he massaged between her shoulder blades. "We'll never get away, Anya. You know that."

"People disappear all the time." She leaned against him, resting her head against his chest, finding minimal solace in rhythm of his strong, steady heartbeat. "Maybe we should go into the federal protection program."

"Do you want that life for your son?"

"Any life is better than none at all." *They could die. All of them. Why didn't he understand?*

"We're too close to ending this. Ending it the right way. Finding the truth about Jeremy's death."

"I don't care."

"Yes, you do." He continued to stroke her back and shoulders. "You care a lot about the truth. About what happened to those villagers in Topaku. About why Jeremy was killed."

He was right. Their quest wasn't about revenge; they were seeking the truth. Only after they found the answers would Jeremy rest in peace.

With a shudder, Anya pulled herself together. She would continue this dangerous charade at Legate. "I need to know my options. I'm going to talk to an attorney."

"I have somebody I can recommend."

"Tomorrow," she said. "I want to see the attorney tomorrow."

"I can make that happen."

He dropped a kiss on her forehead and went to the closet. Calmly, he selected one of his tailored three-piece suits and dressed. His computer played a jazzy tune, and he moved in time to the music as if nothing were wrong. He was humming! How could he be so casual after what had happened this morning? They could have been killed.

Roman appeared to be energized by their nearly lethal encounter. He wasn't scared. His mood had elevated. He seemed happy to be charging into danger.

Anya shook her head. She didn't understand. It must be a testosterone thing.

LATE THAT NIGHT, Roman had Jeremy's laptop up and running. With the help of his own megafunction feminine computer, he scanned through documents and scientific spreadsheets. The good news was that Jeremy saved everything—from his complex research trials to mundane price comparisons on a new garbage disposal. The bad news? Jeremy's filing system made no logical sense to Roman or to his computer.

"Computer," he said, "search for the word *Topaku.*"

"The requested search will take ninety minutes."

"Display as you go," Roman said.

"Unclear request," she replied. If a computer could sound annoyed, she did. "Roman, please clarify."

"As you discover relevant Topaku documents, please display them. One at a time."

Almost immediately, a map of Africa appeared.

"Next," Roman said.

There was another map of Africa. Then a closer map of the area of Topaku. Then a detailed topographic map of the village itself. Apparently, Jeremy had heard of Topaku and was interested enough to take a look at the specific locale.

Did these maps signify anything of importance? The village was geographically isolated in a plateau region amid mountains and forests. No other settlements appeared within a twenty-five-mile radius. There was a river about two miles away. Though Roman didn't see evidence of a sewage system, the village's water needs appeared to be served by a communal well.

One communal well. He thought of Chou Liu's assertion that the water had been poisoned.

Several documents showed other general information, including weather conditions, vegetation, domesticated animals and population. Fifty-three people. Men, women and children. All had died from a virus manufactured in Paris—a virus that was supposedly contained by Legate at Biosafety Level 4.

"Computer, next page."

This was the start of e-mails—dozens of e-mails from concerned biochemists who had heard of the Topaku epidemic or who were involved in virology. Roman paused on one from Aringa, the African scientist who had died in Topaku, the man who had supposedly written the memo that everyone was searching for.

Though this message was nothing more than a friendly, upbeat note to Jeremy, Roman was encouraged. At least Jeremy knew this man.

He stepped back from the computer, realizing that he was reading a letter written from one dead man to another. The everyday inquiries about health and family took on significance. Aringa closed with "Regards to your lovely wife. I hope to meet her someday."

But his days were cut short. His death had come too soon. He continued. "Bless your miracle child." The reference to the miracle of in vitro fertilization clutched at Roman's conscience. He had all the medical information he needed through Maureen's download, and he ought to tell Anya before—

The memo!

As soon as the e-mail popped onto the screen, Roman knew. This was it! He read carefully.

"My friend, excuse my haste…" Several lines followed, in a language Roman couldn't decipher. It had to be Bantu. "I am weak…dizzy…so much death." There was more Bantu, including a reference to Dr. Giddons.

"Computer, print this page," Roman said. "Two copies."

He had to get this page to Anya for translation. He glanced at his wristwatch. Near midnight. He couldn't see her tonight. Tomorrow would have to be soon enough.

ANYA'S VISIT to an attorney in Oakland buoyed her spirits considerably. Her step was light as she left the sleek, well-appointed offices of Forrest, Pickard and Pratt.

When the elevator doors opened on the pink marble lobby in the office building, Roman stood waiting. Though his three-piece black suit was impeccable, he seemed oddly and charmingly disheveled. Excitement flashed in his eyes.

He caught hold of her arm and directed her back into the elevator. "Come with me. There's something I want to show you."

"I can't," she said. "Charlie's out of school in an hour and a half."

As the elevator doors swooshed closed, he said, "I'll get you back on time."

"Thank you for the introduction to Wendy Pratt," she said. "She's wonderful. After looking over the Legate contract, her initial opinion was that Slater can't force me to stay. I'm Charlie's birth mother and his guardian. I can take him anywhere I want."

As she spoke the words, some of the weight lifted from her shoulders. "As for the debt, Slater will have to sue me for it. The way I figure, he'll be out of business before this matter comes to court.''

When the elevator reached the top floor of the twenty-story building, they were the only ones on board. Roman led her around the corner to a door marked Stairs.

''Where are we going?'' she asked.

''A private place.''

They climbed the stairs and stepped out onto a flat roof marked with vents and pipes. A breathtaking vista spread before them, ranging from the city to hillside suburbs to the slate-blue waters of the bay. A canopy of clouds arched above them, and the sunlight fell in shafts of pure light. Overwhelmed by the view, Anya moved nearer to the edge. The wind blew hard, swirling her skirt around her knees.

''We're on top of the world,'' she said. ''I love being up high.''

''I thought of this place when we were in Chinatown,'' he said. ''Sometimes a rooftop is the most private spot in town.''

He slipped his arm around her waist. His mouth claimed hers in a passionate kiss that left her gasping as the fresh, moist wind churned around them. She was part of the sky, at one with the clouds.

Roman led her to a stone bench in the shadow of the roof entry building. Beside it was a matching stone urn filled with mostly dead flowers. ''Other than the fantastic view, why have you brought me here?''

He reached into his coat pocket and produced a single typed sheet. ''The memo.''

Excitement burst inside her chest. This truly was a wonderful day! ''You found it on Jeremy's computer?''

''It was an e-mail.''

She held the edges of the paper tightly, fearful that it

might blow away in a sudden gust. Here was the final proof; everything was falling into place.

After scanning the pieces written in English, she said, "Sounds like Jeremy was friends with Aringa."

"They had a correspondence. Can you translate?"

She concentrated on the Bantu phrases. "When Aringa wrote this, he was ill. *Gonjwa.* That means sickness. He wasn't thinking clearly."

"Which was probably why he lapsed into his native tongue," Roman said.

"He talks about *maji,* water. And a well, *kisima.*" Her grasp of the dialect was enough to understand the basics if not the details. "He believes the Topaku water supply was infected. He says he is sending samples of well water to Giddons." She looked up. "Who's Giddons?"

"He was killed," Roman said. "He worked in the office next door to Jeremy's."

Her high hopes sprang a leak. "That means all his research was destroyed in the explosion. This memo is another dead end."

"Not necessarily. We found Jeremy's laptop. Maybe Giddons saved the information." He took her hand and ran his thumb across her knuckles. "If Giddons found the virus in the water system, it proves that Legate put out a faulty report when they claimed the virus came from the livestock. They lied."

"But does it prove they planted the virus?"

"Close enough." He took the memo from her hand. "I wish we could locate the sample that Aringa shipped to Giddons. That would nail down the case against Legate."

"Surely that evidence has been destroyed."

"Maybe not. Our procedures for handling biohazardous substances are strict."

Roman should know; he'd instituted the policies himself.

And he was also certain that Legate was never authorized by the Center for Disease Control to have a sample of this virus. It had been necessary for the scientists who worked on the vaccine to travel to the Paris lab for their research.

He recalled another odd piece of information. "Everybody at Legate was vaccinated against the virus. It was just before the explosion at Building Fourteen. I remember thinking it was a waste of time because the virus was nowhere near our facility."

"Slater knew," she said. "He knew about this sample."

He agreed with her conclusion, but logic was circumstantial. They needed hard evidence. "We'll look for the sample. And for Giddons's research. This is doable. But it will take time."

"Roman, I don't know how much longer I can stand this waiting."

He tucked a wisp of hair behind her ear. He wished it were that easy to erase the worry from her lovely face. "Slater won't hurt you or Charlie. I'm sure of that."

"And what about you? If anything happens to you…" Her words hung in the air. "Yesterday, you were almost shot."

"But I got away." He smiled, hoping to reassure her. "Without a scratch."

"What about the next time?" Her grasp on his hand tightened. "I've already lost Jeremy, the first man I loved. If I lost you, too…"

Was she saying that she loved him? Throughout the time they'd spent together, those words had not been spoken. Her love? It was almost too much to hope for.

AS ANYA WAITED for proof, her life passed in slow ticks of the clock.

She hung her Christmas decorations, wrapped presents, sang carols.

Roman came to her cottage early on Christmas morning so he'd be there when Charlie awakened. They exchanged gifts, but Anya didn't really get what she wanted: freedom.

Roman followed up on the memo from Aringa. He found confirmation in the mail-room log-in sheets that Giddons received a delivery from Africa at the time of the Topaku epidemic. The biohazardous package went through stringent isolation procedures. Giddons signed it out. He returned it. Then the samples of Topaku well water were gone, presumed lost in the explosion.

Their search ran into another snag. Giddons's next of kin, a brother, had possession of all research papers, but the brother was backpacking through India and couldn't be reached until after the first of the year.

Again, they had to wait.

At midnight on New Year's Eve, Anya raised her glass in a toast. She wished for only one thing: to be far away from Legate. The dry champagne burned her throat.

Two weeks into January, the CIA completed their inspection of the research papers saved by Giddons's brother. They found no record of testing on biohazardous samples from Topaku.

The next day, Anya consulted Wendy, the attorney who advised her to leave Legate subtly. She was Charlie's mother and had every right to remove her son from a situation she deemed unfit.

Unfit? Anya had to laugh. To the rest of the world, her son's life at Legate was a dream come true. A beautiful facility with horseback riding and a swimming pool. Genius instructors. And Charlie loved it—he was thriving.

How could she say this place was unfit for her son? She didn't have evidence. She couldn't prove that Slater was a monster who had killed Charlie's father.

A day before the Chinese New Year parade in San Francisco, Slater and Neville paid her a visit at the cottage. They stood on her doorstep, silhouetted against the dank fog of a cold January day. Unfortunately, she couldn't think of a plausible excuse to turn them away.

They hung their coats on the rack by the door. Apparently, they meant to stay for a while.

"Dr. Neville," she said sweetly, "is everything all right? You look tired."

The dark circles under his eyes almost reached the line of his mustache. "It's been a difficult season," he said.

It was common knowledge that he was under investigation by the American Psychiatric Association and being sued by two parents who had participated in his unethical bonding experiment.

Anya was proud of the part she played in bringing the truth to light. Never again would Dr. Neville manipulate his subjects in such an atrocious manner.

He straightened his necktie. Though his career was swirling down the drain, he was still tidy. "I'm more concerned about you, Anya. This was your first Christmas without your husband."

"Yes," she said simply. The constant ache of grief mingled with all her other anxieties. It was less than a month until the anniversary of Jeremy's death. If it hadn't been for Roman's constant support, she would have crumbled.

"You've lost weight," Slater said critically.

"Having trouble eating?" Neville asked.

As the two men stared at her, she felt as if she were in the Hansel and Gretel fairy tale, confronting the wicked witch who was trying to fatten her up before popping her into the oven.

But she wasn't a helpless victim. "I'm all right."

"I had hoped you would come to see me," Neville said.

"In a professional capacity. You're going through a difficult time."

As if she would ever confide in him. She bit her lower lip, stifling her natural urge to blurt all her hostility. Tersely, she said, "I'm just fine."

She watched as Slater prowled around her cottage. His eyes consumed her belongings. He touched the furniture as if he owned every piece. Which, in fact, he did.

He came to a stop only a few paces from her and stood, staring. "You're lying, Anya."

What did he know? She tensed her muscles, fighting to stay in control. Of course, she lied to him, but she had nothing to be ashamed of. She met his gaze, unflinching. "I'm not a liar."

"You're not fine," he said. "You're distant and confused."

He broke eye contact and turned away from her. A heavy cough racked his body, and he sat in the rocking chair beside the fireplace.

From the pallor of his complexion, she could see that he was ill. But sickness did not diminish his aura of power. He reminded her of a wounded beast, ready to lash out.

"Ever since we had that conversation on Thanksgiving," he said, "you've been avoiding me."

She couldn't deny it.

"I don't like your attitude." His lips drew back from his teeth. "It's not good for Charlie."

You old bastard! Don't tell me what's good for my son. She forced herself to remain silent.

"And yet," Neville put in, "Charlie has a very strong bond with you."

"And you know all about bonding," she said coldly.

"I'm an expert," he said. His chin lifted slightly, giving a nod to his former stature in the field. "Your bond with

Charlie is unusually intense. Like most children his age, his attachment to you—his primary caregiver—is based on dependency. He looks to you for food and shelter and, of course, unconditional love. However, Charlie is also aware of your needs. He's protective, almost to the point of aggression.''

"That sounds normal to me," she said.

"That bond—" Slater broke off to cough. "That bond is the only reason I'm willing to put up with your attitude, Anya."

In spite of his cough, she got the underlying message loud and clear. If it weren't for Charlie, Slater would be happy to get rid of her.

It was ironic that Neville's analysis of Charlie's bonding needs was her only assurance of safety.

The psychiatrist leaned forward, watching her intently. "How does Charlie feel about your relationship with Roman?"

"He's a little jealous."

Slater gave a disbelieving snort. "Charlie doesn't do anything in a small way. He hates Roman."

"No," she said. "Roman is a special link to Charlie's father."

Slater rose from the chair. "The boy likes me better than Roman. As well he should. I've provided him with the intellectual stimulation he needs to reach his full potential. Charlie wouldn't have even been born if it weren't for me. Remember, Anya? The in vitro fertilization. Without me, you wouldn't have gotten pregnant."

Feverish energy sparked from him. His eyes blazed. Anya saw a man who was at the ragged edge of his self-control—a dangerous man who might snap at any moment. He scared her.

"Why did you come here?" she asked.

"To remind you to drop by the clinic tomorrow for your flu shot." He coughed again. "Wish I'd had mine earlier."

No way would she allow herself to be inoculated. From all she'd learned about Legate, they wouldn't hesitate to experiment on their employees. "I don't believe in flu shots."

"You don't have a choice," he said. "It's required. And Charlie will take his shot next week with the other children from the school."

She wouldn't allow that to happen. Her son would never become one of Legate's test studies. Not while there was breath in her body.

As Slater stalked toward the door, Neville bustled after him. "If you feel the need to talk, I'm always available. Goodbye, Anya."

Good riddance. She closed the door behind them.

The Chinese New Year parade in San Francisco was tomorrow night. Chou Liu had promised to contact her, to help her escape. And that was exactly what she meant to do.

Chapter Seventeen

Though Anya had been waiting for the Chinese New Year celebration for what seemed like an eternity, the actual event seemed sudden. She didn't feel prepared for the raucous spectacle of the parade.

She and Charlie were on Kearney Street, watching as an awesome dragon reared his head. Gilded red scales sparkled in the evening mist as the seventy-five-foot-long body snaked through the street. Protectively, she tightened her grip on Charlie's shoulders. He stood in front of her on the curb, and she spoke to the top of his hooded blue sweatshirt. "Are you scared, sweetpea?"

"No way."

She was scared. Terrified, in fact. If only she could be sure she was doing the right thing....

The crowd cheered as skyrockets lit the night. A barrage of firecrackers exploded in a burst of fiery confetti. The dragon gyrated toward her. The long, red snout was so close that Anya could have reached out and slapped it. Abruptly, the beast reared again and danced away.

Charlie craned his neck to look up at her. "I still have the dragon inside the puzzle box that Roman gave me."

He reached into his pocket and held it up so she could see.

"For protection." She nodded her approval. They needed all the protection they could get.

Charlie ducked down and pointed to the black-slippered feet beneath the colorful dragon. "There's probably twenty guys under there."

She mirrored his action, always staying in physical contact. In this crowd, it would be easy to lose track of a small, blond boy who was too smart for his own good.

Following the dragon were dancers waving bright paper lanterns, then paper tigers, then floats and drummers and the lovely Miss Chinatown in her golden crown. The fabulous pageantry barely distracted Anya from her worries. She would have felt a whole lot safer if Roman had been with them.

She'd told him about her desperate plan, and he was supposed to meet her here. But the crowds were huge. Confusion was rampant. All around her was a buzz of conversation. Many spoke staccato Chinese, and she heard the woman behind her say that somebody as tall as Anya should move to the rear.

Oh, good grief! Anya was only five-foot-eight. Not a giantess. But she politely stooped and said, "*Duibugi.*" I'm sorry.

The woman replied, "Xie xie." Thank you.

Amid the noise, she heard a voice, a two-syllable rustling, quiet as the wind. "Anya."

She stood tall. The voice didn't sound like Roman's. Was this the contact from Chou Liu?

"Anya."

Her head swiveled. She searched the crowd, six deep at the curb. Not one face was familiar. *Damn it, Roman. Where are you?*

"Look!" Charlie pointed at a colorful float. The design included leaping, stylized fish.

She bent down again. "Those fish symbolize prosperity and good luck for the New Year."

"So do these." He held out a couple of golden foil-covered chocolate coins that had been pitched into the crowd from the floats. "Boy! Are we going to be lucky!"

"About time."

As another section of the parade moved by, she led Charlie up the steep hill to Chinatown where the festivities would continue into the night. The fact that she hadn't yet been contacted by Chou Liu was beginning to worry her. When they'd first arrived at Chinatown, she'd gone into the building behind Wang Ho's market and knocked on the second-floor apartment door. There had been no answer, and she took to the streets.

"McDonald's!" Charlie cried as he spied the familiar logo on the side of a pagoda.

Anya groaned. Though it might be too much to expect a five-year-old to ask for Szechuan, she couldn't imagine coming to Chinatown for a burger. "How about an egg roll? You like egg rolls."

"McDonald's," he repeated stubbornly.

"We'll walk for a while before we eat." Firmly grasping her son's small hand, she pointed out the brass dragons coiled around the street lamps and Chinese characters on the signs and a multitude of laughing Buddhas. They stopped outside a storefront where a red lacquered dragon took up most of the window display.

"Dragons protect the good guys," Charlie said decisively. "When they see bad guys, they dive down and eat them up in one bite."

"That's so *Jurassic Park*," she said.

He looked up at her with a frown. "Was Daddy one of the good guys?"

"You bet he was. One of the best."

"And Roman? Is he a good guy?"

"I believe so." She peered down at her son. "What do you think?"

"Sometimes he makes me mad. He treats me like a kid."

"Well, Charlie." She tried not to grin. "In actual fact, you are a kid."

"And you always take his side," he accused.

She didn't have a quick and easy answer for that one. Charlie was far too perceptive to be brushed off with a glib reply.

She hadn't told him what might happen tonight, that they might be leaving Legate forever. If Chou Liu didn't show up, she didn't want Charlie knowing any information that he might tell to the wrong person.

She squatted down to her son's eye level. "You've got to trust me, Charlie. About Roman. And about other stuff."

"Like what?"

"Something might happen tonight that…" How could she tell him? She didn't know. "It's a surprise. Anyway, you've got to know that I'm always trying to do the right thing for you."

"Okay." He shrugged. "Can we go to McDonald's? I want fries."

With the parade ended, the streets of Chinatown—which were blocked off to car traffic—filled with boisterous pedestrians. Firecrackers kept up a constant barrage. Sprinkled through the crowd were costumed paraders with elaborate headdresses and bright satin pajamas.

The ceaseless racket hammered at Anya's nerves. There were too many colors, too much activity. It felt as if she and Charlie were trapped inside a whirling kaleidoscope.

"Anya."

She heard the voice clearly and stared across the sea of faces. Then she saw Chou Liu approaching. In his long black coat, the elderly Chinese man seemed like an island of calm in the midst of wild color. A welcoming smile curved his thin lips inside his wispy goatee. *This was really going to happen. She and Charlie were going to escape.*

Dragging her son, she tried to make her way toward Chou Liu. Their progress was slow; a throng of people surged against them.

"Mom? McDonald's is back there."

"Stay with me, Charlie." She stepped off the curb into the street where a bevy of young girls with white lotus flowers in their shining black hair giggled shrilly. As she dodged around them, Anya felt her son's hand being wrenched from her grasp. They were separated. "Charlie!"

Panic blanked out the noise. In a vacuum of fear, Anya spun around. Where was he? If she lost him, she would surely die. It was her worst fear. Colors, lights and faces became a collage of distorted images. "Charlie!"

"I'm right here, Mom." He tugged her jacket. "Jeez!"

She knelt and held his small face between her hands. "Stay with me, Charlie. No matter what happens, stay with me."

Confusion flickered in his eyes. She hadn't meant to frighten him, but this was important and he needed to understand.

"Anya."

The voice was directly behind her. She stood and faced Chou Liu. "Thank God, you're here."

"Come with me," he said. "Your father awaits."

She tried to fall into place beside him, but Charlie balked. "I want fries."

"This is Chou Liu," she said. "We're going with him. We're going to see your grandpa."

"I don't want to."

She tugged at her son's hand. A dancing dragon sepa-

rated her from Chou Liu. The popping of firecrackers co-
alesced into a more solid blast—the heavier thuds of gunfire.

Where did it come from? She whirled.

Chou Liu stared directly at her. The light in his eyes
faded to opaque. His mouth gaped, forming a perfect circle
inside his beard. He clutched at his chest. His legs folded,
and he sank to the pavement.

Still holding Charlie's hand, Anya went down on one
knee beside him. "Someone call an ambulance!"

She tore off her gloves and felt for a pulse at the edge
of his jaw. The skin on his wrinkled throat was hot. His
coat fell open. His white shirtfront was drenched with dark-
red blood.

With an effort, he whispered, "Don't let them take the
boy. Run."

A man in a trench coat squatted beside her. "Step away,
ma'am. There's nothing you can do."

"I know CPR," she said.

"Leave him." His eyes were slits in a cold, impassive
face. "I'll take care of you and your son."

His statement sounded wrong. Why should he be concerned about her and Charlie when a dying man lay before
him?

"It's best," he said, "if you do as I say."

Like hell! She bolted upright. As the man in the trench
coat rose, she shoved hard at his chest. Off balance, he
stumbled backward.

Anya dived into the crowd, pulling Charlie behind her.
They ducked past the revelers, racing toward the nearest
street corner where she turned downhill.

"Mommy, where are we going?"

"Hang on, Charlie."

She lifted him onto her hip and moved with the crowd,

carried along by a churning avalanche of people. Chou Liu told her to run. Someone was after Charlie. She had to run.

At the edge of the crowd, she slipped into a narrow alley, spiderwebbed with fire escapes. If they were caught in here, there would be nowhere to hide. She ran. Charlie, now silent, bounced against her. He was too heavy. Her arms ached. Her sneakers pounded the cobblestones.

At the end of the alley, she glanced over her shoulder, hoping she'd see nothing, hoping there was no reason for fear. But there were shapes in the alley. Someone coming after them, running. A shout reverberated against the narrow brick walls.

She whipped around and faced a man in a black leather jacket. A tall Gypsy man with black hair. "Roman!"

"Get down."

She crouched behind a garbage can, holding Charlie tightly. Then she saw Roman's gun. He aimed and fired three times.

There was gunfire in return. Roman ducked down beside them. "Looks like there are three of them."

Terror stabbed through her. If Charlie hadn't been with her, she would have collapsed in a pathetic heap. But she had to be strong. She had to save her son. "What should we do?"

"Make a run for it. On the street, we've got a better chance of eluding them."

She nodded.

In the dim light, his face was shadowed and hard. He looked fierce enough to handle three gunmen. Or ten. Or twenty.

"I'll lay down some gunfire," he said. "You run. Go uphill. Now."

He stood with legs apart and arms braced like a marksman. He fired. Again and again.

She darted behind him and headed back toward the loud, wild festivities. She'd only gone ten paces when Roman caught up to her. "I'll take Charlie."

Gratefully, she handed over her burden. Her son was too heavy for her to carry while running.

"No," he wailed. "I want Mommy."

"Hang on, Charlie. You've got to be tough."

The boy's small hands balled into fists. "But I'm just a kid."

Anya's heart skipped a beat. It wasn't fair to put Charlie through this. It wasn't right. She ran up beside them as they raced toward the chaotic street scene. "Charlie, do you remember what we were talking about before? About the bad guys?"

He nodded. "Yeah."

"We're the good guys," she said. "We've got to stick together."

"Okay." He clung tightly to Roman as they plunged back into the celebration, hiding in the crowd. There was safety in numbers. People laughing and dancing and talking. Anya stayed close to Roman. Her gaze searched, looking for threats. There were so many distractions and zero probability of finding a policeman in this throng.

As they fought their way through the streets, she lost track of where they were. "Roman, we should go to my mother's house."

"No good," he said. "They'll expect that."

"Then where?"

"Up Nob Hill. To the Ritz-Carlton. We can find a cab there."

On California Street, the crowd began to thin. They were at the edge of Chinatown. Almost magically, they found open space. Fewer people. Less clamor. But was it safe?

Though she couldn't see anyone chasing after them, she sensed the pursuit.

Her labored breath rattled in her throat. She was beyond fatigue, running on sheer tension. Her legs felt as weak as cooked spaghetti, unable to climb this steep hill. If Roman hadn't come along when he did, she hated to imagine what might have happened.

Crossing the street, they dodged the clanging cable car. They were at the edge of the grand Ritz-Carlton Hotel. In half a block they'd be at the front entry. She stumbled, fell on her hands and knees on the pavement. Exhaustion rushed over her. She couldn't go one more pace. "Wait."

Roman was beside her with Charlie in his arms. "We're almost there."

"Gotta catch my breath."

Charlie wriggled free. He wrapped his small arms around her. He was crying. "Mommy, I'm scared."

"Me, too."

Hiccuping through his sobs, he said, "That man was dead."

Gasping, she tried to gather her wits. "He was shot," she said. "I don't know if he was dead."

A dark SUV screeched to a halt at the curb. A man in jeans and a windbreaker leaped out. It was Harrison, the Legate security man who regularly patrolled outside their cottage. "Anya and Charlie," he called out. "Over here. Come with me."

Before she could stop him, Charlie ran toward Harrison—a person he trusted—and the waiting vehicle.

Roman made a desperate lunge and caught hold of Charlie's sweatshirt. The boy fell to the sidewalk.

Anya struggled to her feet and yelled hoarsely, "Charlie, come back here."

But he bounced onto his feet. And he ran toward the

waiting arms of Harrison, who whisked him into the rear of the SUV.

When the security man turned toward her and Roman, she saw that he had a gun in his hand. "Don't make me shoot you, Roman."

"Let the boy go," Roman said. "He belongs with his mother. You know that's the right thing to do."

"Sir, I have my orders."

Roman lifted his own gun, and she slapped his hand down. "Don't shoot. Charlie is in there."

"I was going for the tires."

Harrison slipped into the SUV and slammed the door.

For one more second, Anya stood. Paralyzed. Her worst fear was realized; her son was being taken from her by force.

Unmindful of her own safety, she flung herself toward the SUV door. She yanked frantically at the handle. This couldn't be happening.

The vehicle pulled away from the curb. She didn't let go. She couldn't give up. Not now. "Charlie."

Plummeting down the hill, the SUV picked up speed. She lost her footing, felt herself falling to the pavement. She tumbled. A fierce pain crashed in the back of her head. Everything went black.

IN THE BEDROOM of a house far away from Chinatown, Roman sat at Anya's bedside, holding her hand. She tossed restlessly on the verge of waking up.

Her father, Wade Bouchard, hovered behind him. "She'll be all right," Wade said. "It's a minor concussion."

"Then why isn't she awake? It's been nearly an hour."

"She's afraid." Her father's voice was more clinical than concerned. "I've observed this reaction before. He brain is protecting her from waking up and facing her fear.''

''The fear of losing Charlie.''

''As you and I both know, the boy will be well cared for at Legate.''

''He needs to be with his mother.'' It was taking all Roman's willpower to sit still. He wanted to throttle this old man whose half-witted escape plan had turned into the worst possible disaster.

Wisely, Wade kept his distance. He leaned against the closed door, observing. ''Do you love my daughter?''

''Do you?''

''A fair question.'' Wade's eyebrows lifted to the edge of his high forehead as he considered. ''I haven't been a good father in the traditional sense. But I love my daughter. Everything I do is for Anya. To make a better world for her.''

What a load of idealistic crap! Roman said, ''Kids need a father who can be there for them.''

''Like your father?''

Roman's gut clenched. His father had been there all right. Always ready with a belt or a curse. ''Point taken.''

He turned back toward Anya as her father left the room. Her eyelids squeezed shut. Her limbs twitched as if she were trying to run. Was she reliving their frantic escape?

This was his fault. After all their patience and waiting, he had not arranged a safe escape strategy for her. Instead, she'd been driven by desperation. And everything had gone wrong.

His fingers tightened on her pale, delicate hand. Would she ever forgive him?

Chapter Eighteen

Anya fought her way toward consciousness. Her body ached. The surface of her skin stung as though she'd been attacked by a swarm of wasps who then made a nest inside her head. Constant buzzing assaulted her ears. She had to wake up.

Her eyelids opened, and she saw Roman. His face was smudged, and the knee of his jeans was torn out. He looked as if he'd been through hell. A crooked smile twisted his mouth. "You're awake."

"Where am I?"

"No place special. Don't worry about it."

She could tell that he was trying to protect her, to care for her. Lightly, he wiped her forehead with a cloth. His touch was cool and soothing.

He held out a bottle of water. "Take a sip."

She propped herself up on her elbow and drank. The cool liquid slid down her throat, and the racket inside her head began to fade. "I'm okay, Roman. Please tell me where we are."

"We're still in the city. This house is safe."

In the city. San Francisco. She took another sip of water. She'd come into the city for a specific reason. *Chinatown.* In a flash, she remembered everything. *Charlie!* The water bottle fell from her hand as she struggled to sit up. "Where's my son?"

"Settle down, Anya. You're not strong enough to move around yet."

"I've got to find Charlie."

"He's safe. I'm sure he's safe."

She flung herself out of the bed and stood. A wave of nausea swept over her. She was too dizzy to take even one step. But she had to. From somewhere deep inside, she found the fortitude to remain on her feet.

She remembered the chase. The gunfire. The Legate SUV that carried her son away. "He's with Slater."

Roman stood at her elbow. "And Slater would never harm the boy."

"How the hell do you know that?" A blinding pain squeezed her eyes shut. "He killed my husband. He could kill…"

Words failed her. Her knees buckled. Roman held her as she sank onto the bed.

"Lie back," he said.

Coherent thought began to weave through her brain. This time, Slater had gone too far. His men killed Chou Liu. Legate security had taken Charlie from her at gunpoint. "We need to call the police."

"I advise against it," Roman said.

"But this isn't a complicated conspiracy. There's no lack of evidence. Chou Liu was killed."

"Did you see someone pull the trigger?" His voice wasn't accusatory but gentle. And a little sad.

"There was a guy in a trench coat."

"Could you identify him?"

Muddled images rocked through her brain. "There were dragons. Paper lanterns. And pretty girls with white flowers in their hair."

But she hadn't actually witnessed the murder. Despite the headache, her mind became clear. "Maybe I didn't witness the murder, but I saw them take Charlie. It was Harrison, the guy who patrols outside the cottage. I can tell the police exactly what happened."

"It's still our word against theirs," Roman said. "All they did was take Charlie home. To Legate."

"But I'm his mother." No matter what else had happened, no one could deny her that right. "I want my son back with me. The police have to help me."

Roman went down on one knee before her. He took her hands in his. "We'll get Charlie back. Losing him is not an option."

Her gaze sank into his dark tawny eyes, and she saw sympathy and caring. He wanted to help her. What was standing in his way? "What is it, Roman?"

"There's something I have to tell you." He glanced down, buying time before he spoke. His reluctance was palpable.

"More bad news," she said.

"Very bad."

She couldn't imagine anything worse than what she was feeling right now. "Go ahead."

He raised her hands to his lips and brushed a kiss across her knuckles, reminding her of the first day she saw him at Legate when he pretended to be flirting with her. Even then, it wasn't a game. She and Roman were connected. Their relationship was the only positive thing to come from this whole experience.

"I should have seen this from the start," he said. "I should have guessed."

"What are you talking about?"

"Six years ago, you and Jeremy came to Legate, hoping for a miracle."

"And it happened," she said. "The in vitro fertilization was successful. I conceived my son."

"You conceived," he said gently. "But Charlie is not your son."

The enormity of his statement stunned her. Behind her eyes, she felt darkness rising like a thunderhead.

Roman continued. "You were implanted with a fertilized egg from a different genetic father and mother. In effect, you were a surrogate mother."

She wouldn't believe this. "That's a lie."

He knelt before her, his hands holding hers. "I wish, with all my heart, that I was lying."

"You have proof?"

"I obtained your medical records along with those of Jeremy and Charlie. The blood types didn't match up."

"Blood typing is an inexact science."

"I did the DNA," he said. "Neither you nor Jeremy are the biological parents of Charlie."

She remembered finding those medical charts in Roman's bedroom. She hadn't known what he was looking for, but she hadn't followed up because she trusted him. He was one of the good guys. And she was…not Charlie's mother.

Receiving this information was like hearing a death sentence. Her world stopped turning. "How could this happen?"

"The other fertility doctors you and Jeremy went to were correct in their diagnosis. There was no way—as a couple—you could have had a child. Possibly, Neville selected you for his bonding experiments."

She remembered the psychiatrist's questions, his insistence that she and Charlie had formed an unusually successful bond. But Neville hadn't told her that she was not the biological mother.

It didn't matter to her. Did she love Charlie? Yes! Did he love her? Yes! "He's still my son."

"Not in the eyes of the legal system," Roman said. "You and Charlie are not genetically related."

"Who are the biological parents?" An even more terrible thought occurred to her. "Not Slater?"

"No," Roman said quickly. "That was the first thing I checked out. Slater has severe allergies he didn't want to pass along to the next generation."

"Then who?"

"When the fertilization experiments were being conducted, several people at Legate donated sperm and eggs. Charlie was made from the best of the best, created from the DNA of genius parents."

"He was an experiment." A sob escaped her lips. Her world was falling apart. God help her! She knew Roman spoke the truth. She accepted every word.

In creating her son, Fredrick Slater had been playing God. He made Charlie a genius. That was why Slater took such an interest in the boy, why he insisted that Charlie be part of the Legate schooling. Slater was raising a test-tube baby of his own design, grooming him to take over Legate.

She slumped. All the fight drained from her limbs. "I don't have the right to go to the police. Charlie isn't really my son."

"Don't give up." Roman sat beside her on the bed. Though she knew his arm was around her, she couldn't feel his touch. Her body was numb.

Roman continued. "There'll be a legal battle. But, in the end, you'll have Charlie back."

"You can't promise…" Her voice faded. She fell back on the pillows. Slowly, she stretched out her legs, resting on a bed of shattered hopes. Her eyelids closed. "I want to sleep. Forever."

"Of course," Wade said, "I knew."

Roman glanced over his shoulder toward the bedroom door where Anya had been sleeping for hours. One of Wade's companions—a medical doctor whose reputation was world renowned—had been keeping an eye on her, monitoring her vital signs.

Apart from bruises and a minor concussion, there was nothing wrong with her health. Except, perhaps, for a broken heart.

He turned toward her father, who sat across a scarred wood kitchen table. Wade nursed a cup of coffee. Like Roman, he hadn't slept. It was four o'clock in the morning.

"How did you know?" Roman asked.

"As soon as I heard Anya was going to Legate, I was suspicious."

"Why?" He'd been working at Legate when the fertilization experiments were ongoing, and he hadn't suspected a thing. "How did you know?"

"I'll admit that Legate has accomplished some good works in the realm of science and politics. But I always knew Slater was ruthless," Wade said. "Fredrick Slater is living proof of Lord Acton's adage."

Roman quoted, "Power tends to corrupt. Absolute power corrupts absolutely."

"As Legate grew in power and reputation, Slater became convinced that he was above the law, above any retribution. Nothing could stand in his way. And he wanted a suitable heir."

"Charlie," Roman said. Fredrick Slater had genetically engineered his successor.

"When I heard my daughter was going to Legate to try an experimental fertilization technique, I tried to dissuade her. Even talked to Claudette." When he mentioned his ex-wife's name, his blue eyes—exactly the same shade as

Anya's—twinkled. "She told me to go to hell. In no un-
certain terms. Claudette has always been feisty."

"To say the least," Roman agreed.

"After Charlie was born," Wade said, "I called in a few
favors from docs I knew. I got DNA tests for the boy, Anya
and Jeremy. And I knew."

He poured more coffee from the carafe into his cup.
Carefully, he measured exactly one level teaspoon of sugar,
added it and stirred. His precision reminded Roman that
Wade Bouchard had, at one time, been a cutting-edge scientist—somewhat of a genius in his own right.

"Anya and Jeremy were good candidates for this experiment," Roman said with disgust. "Both highly intelligent.
No one was surprised when Charlie's IQ tested off the
charts."

"I intended to tell her," Wade said. "But when I visited
her and saw how much she adored the child, I couldn't."

Roman understood. He was guilty of the same reluctance. He'd known the secret of Charlie's birth for nearly
two months and had said nothing to Anya. He didn't want
to hurt her. "Do you think Jeremy knew?"

Wade shrugged. "Jeremy was a biochemist, familiar
with medical science. He knew the facts, the astronomical
odds against his ability to reproduce. He chose to believe
in a miracle and didn't care about the truth."

A dangerous thought occurred to Roman. "Maybe he
learned the truth. Maybe that's why Jeremy was murdered."

Wade looked up sharply. "I think it's time, Roman Alexander, for you and me to lay all our cards on the table."

"You're talking about the Topaku epidemic."

"That's right."

Roman leaned back in the uncomfortable ladder-back
chair. After a year of undercover work with the CIA, he

never expected to be across the table from Wade Bouchard, a reputed crackpot who danced at the edges of world conspiracies. "Why should I trust you?"

Wade barked a laugh. "I'm all you've got, Roman. You want to get Charlie back from Legate, right?"

Roman nodded. "I want Anya and her son to be together."

"You think the CIA is going to help?" Wade sneered. "You think they give two hoots about Anya?"

Maureen cared. Roman knew the red-haired agent had a heart that was as soft as a marshmallow. But she didn't give the orders. And the CIA wanted evidence to use in court. They wanted an iron-clad case against Legate before they pressed charges.

"Face it," Wade said. "There isn't time to wait for the CIA to act."

From behind his back, Roman heard the creak of a floorboard. He turned and saw Anya.

"I want my son," she said. "Now."

Though she'd been sleeping, her eyes were ringed with shadows. Her complexion was as pale as her hair. But her spine was stiff and her gait determined as she stalked across the small room and pulled out a chair from the table.

"How much did you overhear?" her father asked.

"Enough to know that you think Jeremy might have been killed because he knew about Charlie's biological parents." She reached for the carafe and poured herself a half-cup of coffee. "Let's start there."

Roman felt like he should say something to her. An apology. He ought to tell her that he was sorry for keeping the secret of Charlie's birth. Even more, he was sorry that he had to be the one who told her.

When he glanced across the table at Wade, Roman saw his own thoughts reflected.

Neither of them knew how to deal with this woman who had been through the loss of her husband and was now facing separation from her child. Nothing they could say would make it right.

"Let's get one thing straight." She stared coldly at each of them in turn. "Charlie is my son. It takes more than a DNA test to determine parentage. I'm his mother. He belongs with me."

Her courage touched him. "What do you want us to do?"

"Get my son back."

Solemnly, he nodded. He would do whatever it took to meet her demand. He'd get Charlie back or die trying.

"If we go through legal channels," Wade said, "it might take a while. But I know several good attorneys who—"

"Not good enough," she said. "I want him back today."

"It's impossible," her father said. "Charlie's at Legate, and you both know that place is a fortress. Am I right, Roman?"

"Yes," he said.

"We'll deal with first things first," Wade said. "We need to clear up the mystery surrounding the Topaku epidemic. Roman, I believe we were about to put our cards on the table."

"You first," Roman said. "How do you know so much about what happened there?"

"I have a source inside Legate," Wade said. "Don't ask for the name. I won't give it to you."

"You call this putting our cards on the table?"

"We're talking about Topaku," her father said.

"Fine. Let's deal with this."

With Roman doing most of the talking, they came up with a direct line of events. The virus was created and isolated in a Paris laboratory. They contacted Legate, supposedly to create a vaccine and safe handling procedures. But the real agenda for Legate was to perform a test, to find out if the virus was suitable as a biochemical weapon.

"Who are your sources?" Roman asked.

"Scientists who are now affiliated with SCAT. Because of their politics, the CIA doesn't consider these men to be reliable witnesses."

Then the village of Topaku was selected as the site for testing. "It fit the criteria for a controlled test," Roman said. "An isolated village with a single water supply."

The African biochemist, Aringa, occasionally worked for Legate on biochemical projects. He was in Topaku when the virus appeared in what looked like a spontaneous outbreak. But the arrival of the Legate staff with a vaccine caused Aringa to suspect the virus might have been introduced as a test through the water supply. He sent the memo to Jeremy. And he sent the specimens to Dr. Giddons at Legate.

"And that's where the trail ends," Roman said. "The specimens were lost."

Wade asked, "What project was Giddons working on at the time the samples arrived?"

"Wheat," Roman said. "He was working on a bio-engineered strain of wheat that would grow faster and stronger. At the time the samples arrived, Giddons wasn't even at Legate."

"Which would have made it easy for someone else to take those samples and destroy them," Wade said.

"That didn't happen." Roman knew Legate procedures inside and out. "When biohazardous samples are logged in through the mail room, they are delivered immediately to the proper lab and put into secure storage. In this case, refrigerated. They were in there for days, waiting for Giddons to return. Records show that he checked them out and returned them.''

''But they're gone now,'' Anya said. Disappointment was evident in her voice. ''We have no way of proving they ever existed.''

''Except for a note on a log-in sheet,'' Roman said.

The three of them sat in silence. Outside the apartment, the sun was rising. Dawn light splintered through the blinds.

Stiffly, Wade rose from the table and stretched. ''I'll make more coffee.''

Roman's gaze went across the table toward Anya. Though they had been together many nights, making love in his bedroom, they seldom shared the early-morning hours. She always had to leave him and hurry back to the cottage so she'd be there when Charlie got up.

He wanted that pattern to change—never to be apart from her again. He wanted to spend every night holding her and wake up every morning to see her pale blond hair spread across his pillows.

''I've got it!'' Wade stepped away from the sink, leaving the water running. ''We have proof, irrefutable proof.''

A wild light shone from his blue eyes. Either he was brilliant or crazy as a loon.

Leaning both hands on the table, he explained, ''Suppose Giddons did the tests and found evidence of the virus in the water. Roman, what would he do next?''

''He'd report his findings to Slater.''

''And Slater would know that these findings could prove that the virus was purposely introduced in the village.''

Roman nodded. ''If you're suggesting that Slater blew up the building to kill Giddons and destroy the specimens, I can believe it. But where's the proof?''

''Dr. Giddons received a strange memo from Aringa. Most of it was in a language he didn't understand.''

''Right.''

''What if he was careless in his handling of the specimen?'' Wade posed the question like a professor, waiting for his students to figure out the truth. ''What if he became infected with the virus?''

''It's possible,'' Roman said.

''From what I understand,'' Wade said, ''this virus from the Filoviridae group is not particularly virulent. Infection comes either from livestock by-products or, in this case, through direct and prolonged exposure. For instance, working closely together in a laboratory.''

Roman remembered his last moments with Jeremy. He was ill, coughing. He'd said that there was something going around. Other people were sick. *They had been infected with the virus.*

''Slater had to blow up the entire building,'' Roman said, ''to prevent the spread of the virus.''

''And I'll bet there were inoculations given at Legate at just that time. The vaccine.''

''You're right,'' Roman said.

''Wait a minute,'' Anya said. She scowled at both of them. ''I still don't see what this proves.''

''Jeremy had the virus,'' Roman said. ''But the virus was never supposed to be at the Legate facility. The only way he could have caught it was through the sample. That's our proof.''

Realization spread slowly across her face. ''Evidence of the virus is still in his remains. You want me to exhume my husband's body.''

It was a painful decision, but she made it quickly. ''Roman, please inform Maureen of our conclusions. I'm sure the CIA can prepare any paperwork I need to sign for the exhumation.''

"You see," Wade said, "this will all work out. Legate will be closed down, and you'll have Charlie back before you know it."

"That's not soon enough."

Her eyes flashed as she turned toward Roman. "If anyone can get past Legate security, it's you."

"I hope you're not suggesting a break-in."

"I'm not suggesting anything," she said. "I'm demanding. You lied to me, and you used me. Because you kept me in the dark, I wasn't prepared for what happened in Chinatown. Damn it, Roman. I lost my son. Now you're going to help me get him back."

He didn't try to defend himself against her anger, but he didn't back down, either. He maintained eye contact with her, wishing he would see a glimmer of forgiveness. But there was nothing of the sort. She despised him.

Slowly, he nodded. "I'll get Charlie back."

"And when this is over," she said, "when my son is with me, I never want to see or speak to you again."

Chapter Nineteen

At 7:48 p.m., Roman crept along the rocky shoreline approaching the sandy stretch of Legate bay-front property where he did his morning run. Light from the rising moon rippled across the dark water, and silver-tipped waves splashed against the rugged black rocks. Freezing droplets dampened his jeans, and he wished he'd worn a wet suit.

Following behind him, Anya breathed in sharp gasps. She shouldn't be here. She wasn't in shape to make this assault. But there was no way he could convince her to stay behind.

When he reached the rocks at the edge of the beach, he paused and checked his wristwatch. Anya scrambled up beside him.

"Eight minutes," he said.

Timing was crucial. At precisely eight o'clock, Maureen had arranged to cut the power to Legate. Though a backup generator kicked on within seconds, the computerized security system would be disabled for at least twenty minutes—time enough for Roman and Anya to rescue Charlie.

Another distraction would come at ten minutes after eight when Maureen and four other agents, including two experts from the Center for Disease Control, would approach the front door of the Legate mansion with a warrant to search records in the medical facility and to check the biohazardous storage systems.

Slater would be kept busy, dealing with them.

In theory, Roman and Anya would get away clean before the security system was fully operational.

"Tell me again," Anya whispered. "What do we do at eight o'clock?"

"Cross the beach. Climb the eighty-seven stairs leading up the cliffside. And go to the cottage."

"Which is how far?"

"A mile and a quarter."

He looked directly into her pale face, which was framed by the black knit cap she wore to cover her light blond hair. Though he could see her determination, he wasn't sure that she was physically up to this challenge. Even with his speed, Roman would be hard-pressed to make this rescue within the twenty-minute limit.

"It's better if you stay here," he said. "When the security system comes back on, they'll be able to pinpoint our location."

"Charlie is my son," she said. "I can do this."

"Look, I know you're mad at me, but—"

"'Mad' doesn't begin to describe the way I feel about you."

"You've got to trust me to handle this. If you run into trouble, it's dangerous. Both for you and for Charlie."

"I won't make a mistake," she said.

This was her decision, and he had to accept it. In truth, he found her determination to be admirable. She was brave and strong, everything he'd ever wanted in a mate. As he studied her fine features, memorizing the lift of her eyebrow and the jut of her chin, Roman refused to believe their relationship was over. She was more precious to him than air.

He unholstered his handgun. ''There's one thing I have to say before we go charging in there.''

''Don't,'' she said.

''This might be my last chance to tell you,'' he said. ''I didn't keep the secret of Charlie's birth to be cruel. I meant to spare you more pain.''

''Why?''

''Because I care about you, Anya.'' He lifted her chin. ''I love you.''

Before she had a chance to respond, he checked his watch. ''Eight o'clock. Let's go.''

He eased around the rocks and onto the edge of the beach. His custom-made running shoes hit the sand. In a sprint, he raced to the stairs.

She'd already fallen behind, and he waited for ten valuable seconds for her to catch up. Then he started to climb. Eighty-seven wooden steps, slick with mist. Roman knew to be careful with his footing.

At the top, he ducked down. Though the security system ought to be shut off, he wasn't taking any chance of being seen.

Anya wheezed as she climbed. Three steps from the top, her foot slipped. She caught the railing before she fell more than a couple of stairs, but she gave a muffled cry.

''Are you hurt?'' he whispered.

''Twisted my ankle.''

Roman counted this accident as a lucky break. Now, she'd have to stay out of danger's way. ''Climb back down. Go around the rock ledge and wait.''

''I can make it.''

''You can't. You'll jeopardize the whole rescue. Go back.''

"Roman?"

"What?"

"Do you really love me?"

"With all my heart."

He took off at a dead run. Patrolling security guards would be watching the path where Roman usually did his morning exercise, but he knew where they were posted. These grounds were familiar territory. He knew every tree, every rock.

An armed guard approached, and Roman dived behind a thicket. He wouldn't be caught. Couldn't be. Too much was riding on this escape.

A full minute elapsed. The only flaw in Roman's plan was his assumption that Charlie would be at the cottage. If the boy was being held in the gray stone mansion or one of the outbuildings, there wasn't enough time to conduct a search.

But Roman knew Slater and Neville well enough to predict what they would do. They didn't want to upset Charlie more than necessary. They would understand the importance of leaving him in familiar surroundings, allowing him to sleep in his own bed. Very likely, they'd invented a story about how his mother would be coming to see him very soon.

The security guard moved on.

Roman was on his feet, running again.

Light shone through the windows of Anya's cottage. Someone was there with Charlie. He prayed it wasn't Slater. With light steps, Roman approached the porch.

"Don't move."

He heard the click of a safety being removed from a handgun. He stopped and wheeled around. It was Harrison. "You've come for Charlie," he said.

"The boy belongs with his mother."

In spite of what had happened in San Francisco, Roman didn't believe that Harrison was a mindless thug. Over the months, the security guard had gotten to know Anya and Charlie. He liked them, cared about them.

Harrison cocked his arm, then lowered his pistol. "Tell Anya I'm sorry."

Roman slipped through the front door of the cottage. Claudette was alone in the front room. For the first time since Roman had known this severe woman, she looked disheveled. Her hand trembled as she reached toward him. "Is Anya safe?"

"She'll be fine. As soon as her son is with her again."

Charlie clattered down the stairs. When he saw Roman, his eyes narrowed. "What did you do to my mommy?"

"She's waiting for you, Charlie. Let's go."

"No," he shouted. "I hate you."

His arm drew back, and he threw something at Roman. It was the small dragon from the first puzzle box.

Roman picked up the dragon and stashed it in his pocket. It wouldn't hurt to carry a dragon charm for protection. "Come with me, Charlie. I'm taking you to your mom."

"No! Mr. Slater says you're bad."

Roman didn't have time for explanations. The minutes were ticking away. The security system would be back on.

Claudette marched up to the boy. "Listen to me, young man. You're going with Roman. Right this minute."

"But Mr. Slater says—"

"Mr. Slater is an ass," Claudette snapped. "Now go."

Roman scooped the boy up. Charlie was fighting him, wriggling to get away. So much for a stealthy escape.

Out on the porch, they saw an amazing sight. Anya rode toward them. She was bareback on the palomino mare named Pegasus—Charlie's favorite from the stables.

Pride swelled in Roman's chest as he watched her approach. She rode bareback like a champ, expertly snapping the reins. Her tenacity amazed him. This was one hell of a woman.

"Mommy!"

"Get up here, sweetpea."

Roman lifted the boy onto the horse. Their plan had been to escape via the same route they used to enter. But the horse couldn't go down the stairs to the beach. "Go to the front gate," he said. "Maureen will be there."

Charlie clung to her, and she planted a quick kiss on top of his head before glancing down at Roman. "There's room here for one more."

"You'll go faster alone," he said. "I'll see you later."

"I want you to be with me," she said.

As she looked down at him, Anya was fully aware of the double meaning in her words. She wanted Roman to be with her and Charlie—now and forever. Though she hadn't planned to forgive him, she couldn't dismiss these long months together. She couldn't honestly deny their closeness.

When Roman spoke of love, she believed him. He'd never meant to hurt her. He was a good man trapped in a bad situation.

"Please," she said, "be with us."

Instead of leaping onto the horse behind her, he took the reins and tugged. Roman took off at a quick jog and Pegasus stayed behind him.

Jostling on the back of the horse, Anya clenched with her knees. The pain in her ankle was something fierce, and she fought it. Her arm wrapped tightly around her child. *He was her son.* "Hold on to the mane, Charlie."

At the edge of the mansion, they came to a halt. Through the shadows, she saw the outline of several security guards. There seemed to be a commotion at the front entryway.

Roman came back to her. ''We have to walk from here.''

Her ankle throbbed. It wasn't broken but badly sprained, and she wasn't anxious to put weight on it. ''Can't we ride on through? The guards won't shoot at us. They know us.''

He glanced toward Charlie. ''That's a chance we don't want to take.''

After Roman helped Charlie down to the ground, he held up his arms toward her. Moonlight glistened in his black hair. In spite of everything that had happened, his lips curved in an encouraging smile.

She slid into his arms. This was where she belonged. *He was her mate.*

Then her foot touched the ground and she winced.

''Lean against me,'' Roman whispered. ''We'll go through the back door.''

Hobbling, she made her way forward. Charlie was right beside her. ''Mommy, you're hurt.''

''Hush, Charlie. We have to be quiet.''

Bright lights illuminated the rear of the mansion, and she knew their final approach would be dangerous. As if to underline her thought, sirens began to wail. The security system had come back on. Video cameras would be operational.

She saw an armed guard move to stand in front of the rear door to the mansion.

Roman backed off. ''We've got to hide.''

''The maze,'' Charlie said.

The tall hedges were right beside them. Though winter had stripped the leaves, it was a good hiding place. ''He's right,'' Anya said.

Roman nodded to the small boy. ''Lead the way.''

Without a single mistake, Charlie directed them to the center of the maze. Anya sat on the edge of the marble fountain and reached down to the cold water. She splashed a handful onto her face and pulled the cap off her head. When she looked up, she saw Charlie watching her. His gray eyes were solemn, concerned. "You're going to be okay, Mommy."

She gathered him into her arms. "So are you, sweetpea."

"Don't leave me, Mommy. Not ever again."

"Never again," she said.

Standing on tiptoe, Roman peeked over the hedges. "Something's happening."

She heard the shouts, the sound of people running. Were they coming here?

Roman took his cell phone from his pocket. He punched in a number. In a whisper, he said, "Maureen. We're coming through the mansion from the back. Don't leave the front door."

He disconnected the call and turned to Anya. "If we make it to the front, we're home free."

The distance was less than twenty yards, but it seemed like miles. She didn't know if she could go twenty steps. But she had to. It was the only way.

Roman peered over the hedge again. "They've left the door unguarded. Let's go."

She stumbled a few steps into the maze, tried to go faster. It was impossible. Her ankle throbbed. "Go on without me. Take Charlie."

"Like hell," Roman said. He lifted her off her feet with one arm under her knees and the other around her back. She felt the pistol in his right hand. With her arms around his neck, she held on for dear life.

She whispered, "Stay with us, Charlie."

"Okay, Mom."

With Roman carrying her, they moved swiftly, emerging from the maze. Incandescent lights shone brightly across dead grass and the wide flagstone patio. But Roman didn't hesitate. He charged toward the mansion. At the rear door, he pressed his thumbprint against the locking device and turned the handle. The door opened.

They were inside the mansion. Still carrying her, Roman strode through the wide hallway leading to the front foyer. They were going to make it! Anya's heart beat faster. In a few more steps, this seemingly endless nightmare would be over. Finally, they'd be free from Legate.

Then she saw Slater. Her brief illusion of safety shattered, and she gasped in horror. He stood directly in their path. In his hand was a small pistol.

"That's far enough," he said.

From where they stood, Anya could see the edge of the front foyer. She could hear the echo of a heated discussion.

"Give it up," Roman said. "You've lost, Slater."

"I never lose."

Roman released her legs and let Anya's legs slip to the floor. His gun hand remained hidden behind her back, and she remembered how she'd managed to distract Peter Bunch. There was no chance of such a diversion with Slater.

"In here," Slater said as he pushed open the door to the dining room. "Move."

Roman nodded to her. "Do as he says."

"A wise decision," Slater said. "There's no reason for any of you to be hurt."

Roman supported Anya as she hobbled into the high-ceilinged dining room filled with chairs and tables of varying sizes. There was space to maneuver, but he knew that Anya wasn't capable of moving quickly. He helped her to a chair.

Slater closed the door behind himself, and a cool silence descended. Despite three sets of French doors that led onto the rear patio, this room was well soundproofed. A gunshot would be heard but not a cry for help.

As Slater faced them, he coughed. He looked like hell. His shirt collar was open, revealing a swelling below his jawline. His eyes were red-rimmed, and his complexion had taken on a waxy sheen. Roman recognized the symptoms. This was the way Jeremy had looked when he'd been infected.

"Oh, my God," he whispered. Slater had the disease. "What have you done?"

"Legate is my creation." His voice was hoarse. "I built this place from a pathetic little think tank to a world-renowned power. My power."

Insane with fever, he was raving. Every step he took was an obvious effort.

"You need medical help," Roman said.

"You'd like that, wouldn't you? Lock me away in a hospital bed so you could take over?" Slater reached inside his vest pocket and produced a vial. "This is it! The thing you've all been searching for. Samples from Topaku's water supply."

"Where was it?"

"My wall safe. Behind the Degas."

How could a man like Slater be so foolish? He knew how to handle a biohazardous substance. "Why didn't you get rid of it?"

"It's mine," he said. "I've carried it with me. I'll infect this whole place. Close it down. Doesn't matter anymore. If I'm not here, Legate is worthless."

"There's still time," Roman said. "You could—"

"Quiet!" His gaze dropped, and his fierce red eyes focused on Charlie. "Come over here, my boy. Don't be afraid."

"You're sick," Charlie said.

"But you won't catch it," he said. "When you first came here, I had you vaccinated."

"How could you?" Anya demanded. "I never gave permission."

"So many things happened at the school," Slater said. "You didn't have a clue."

He leaned on a tabletop, breathing heavily.

"You didn't vaccinate yourself," Roman said. He knew Slater's weakness from the medical information. "You couldn't because of your allergies."

"An accurate deduction." He stood a little straighter. "But I will recover. There is a treatment. We discovered it after it was too late to save those unfortunate souls at Topaku."

"There was a cure?" Anya stiffened in the chair. "You could have cured Jeremy, but you killed him instead."

"I couldn't leave evidence." Slater's sneer was ghastly. "Come, Charlie. You and I are going to take a trip. We'll go to wonderful places. We'll continue your education."

Charlie took a few steps toward him. He planted his feet and raised an accusing finger. "Did you kill my daddy?"

"You understand, don't you? For the greater good."

"Charlie," Roman said, "I want you to do what I say. Run to the far end of the room and hide."

He turned and faced Roman. Tears coursed down his round cheeks, and his lower lip trembled.

"Please," Anya said. "Hide, Charlie."

"Don't listen to them," Slater said. "You don't like Roman. He wants to take you away. You'll never reach your full potential."

Charlie's small hands rose to the middle of his chest. He gave a thumbs-up signal. Quick as a jackrabbit, he ran and disappeared amid the chairs and tables in the huge, open room.

Roman stepped in front of Anya. He raised his own gun and pointed at Slater. "Drop your weapon."

Slater coughed. With his free hand, he wiped the sweat from his brow. "You're aware of what I'm holding in my hand, aren't you? This small handgun is a marvel of physics. I can shoot through you and kill Anya, as well."

Roman had seen the prototype for this gun. He knew Slater wasn't lying.

"I'll do it," Slater said. "I have nothing to lose."

"Wrong," Roman said. "Shoot us in cold blood, and you lose your humanity. What happened to you? You built an empire based on the greater good."

"I believe that." He swayed precariously, but his gun hand remained steady. "Everything I do benefits mankind. You're not capable of seeing the big picture. Your mind is too small."

Behind his back, the dining room door swung open, framing Jane Coopersmith.

Slater barely glanced at her. "Good. You're here. Find the boy. He's hiding among the tables."

"I know," Jane said. "I know everything."

She opened the door wider. Wade Bouchard followed her inside.

"Dad!" Anya shouted.

Wade hadn't been part of their assault plans. It wasn't his way. He preferred to work from the shadows. But not this time. He stepped inside. With his fists on his hips and his chest thrust out, he looked around as if he owned the place.

"Well, now," Wade said. "It appears that we've trapped the grizzly in his cave."

"Come closer," Slater beckoned. "Touch my hand."

"Don't do it," Jane warned. "He's got the virus."

Wade kept his attention on Slater. "What was your plan?

I assume you intended to infect the entire compound, possibly to infect the rats and allow them to spread the disease. You planned to escape with the boy, didn't you?''

"You're an old fool."

"Possibly," Wade conceded. "But I'm not the one who's allowed himself to be apprehended."

"They'll never take me." Slater turned the gun toward himself. The barrel pointed at his temple. There was enough firepower in that weapon to blow his head off.

Roman knew it was now or never. He didn't want Slater to commit suicide. That fate was too easy. Slater should suffer for the pain and death he'd caused. He should be punished for Jeremy's murder.

Taking aim, Roman fired his pistol. He hit Slater's arm, and the powerful handgun clattered to the floor.

Slater staggered but remained standing. Bloodied but unbowed. True evil was hard to kill.

Two men in Haz-Mat suits stormed into the dining room. As they took Slater into custody, whisking him out of the room, Maureen entered and immediately took charge.

"Nobody leaves," she said. "We're under quarantine."

Roman knelt beside Anya and took her hand. "Quarantine? Looks like we're stuck here again."

She shook her head slowly. "I've pretty much accepted that there is no escape from Legate."

"Or from me," he said. "I'm always going to be with you."

Charlie ran up beside them. He buried his face on her shoulder.

"We're going to be okay, sweetpea. We're safe now."

With one arm, Anya hugged her son. From the other side, Roman embraced her. They formed a small tableau of calm in the chaos of the dining room where Wade loudly protested the quarantine. Jane Coopersmith hovered silently at his side. And Maureen directed the other agents and the officials from the Center for Disease Control.

With a sigh, Anya leaned against Roman's chest. Exhausted, she could feel the last reserves of strength leaving her body. She tilted her head to look up at him. "Are we having fun yet?"

The smile that lit his handsome face was a wonderful sight. She hugged Charlie a bit tighter. This was her family. This was what she wanted.

"I love you, Anya."

"And I love you, Roman."

Charlie piped up. "Roman, can I have my dragon back?"

He placed the small statue in Charlie's hand. "It was good protection."

"Yeah," Charlie said. "I don't hate you anymore. You can take care of me and Mommy."

"We all take care of each other."

Wade came toward them. He bellowed, "Where's my grandson?"

"Me?" Charlie asked.

"Yes, you." He grasped the boy's hand. "I hear you're pretty smart. Let's talk epidemiology."

"Okay." Before leaving Anya's side, Charlie kissed her cheek. Then he turned to his grandfather. "I like -ologies. Biology and virology and anthology."

"Anthology?" Wade gave him a puzzled look.

"Study of ants," Charlie said with assurance.

Anya smiled into Roman's eyes. She felt a warmth inside her heart that spread through her body. This had been a long, hard road to happiness. Now that she'd found it, she would never let go. "Tell me again."

"I love you?"

"And I love you."

She knew, without fear or doubt, that they would be together. Forever.

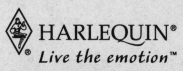

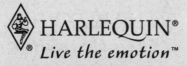

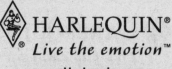

HARLEQUIN® *Super*ROMANCE®

Men of the True North—
Wilde and Free

The Wilde Men

Homecoming Wife
(Superromance #1212)
On-sale July 2004

Ten years ago Nate Wilde's wife, Angela, left and never came back.
Nate is now quite happy to spend his days on the rugged trails of
Whistler, British Columbia. When Angela returns to the resort
town, the same old attraction flares to life between them. Will
Nate be able to convince his wife to stay for good this time?

Family Matters
(Superromance #1224)
On-sale September 2004

Marc was the most reckless Wilde of the bunch. But when an
accident forces him to reevaluate his life, he has trouble accepting
his fate and even more trouble accepting help from Fiona Gordon.
Marc is accustomed to knowing what he wants and going after it.
But getting Fiona may be his most difficult challenge yet.

A Mom for Christmas
(Superromance #1236)
On-sale November 2004

Aidan Wilde is a member of the Whistler Mountain ski patrol, but
he has never forgiven himself for being unable to save his wife's
life. Six years after her death, Aidan and his young daughter still
live under the shadow of suspicion. Travel photographer Nicola
Bond comes to Whistler on an assignment and falls for Aidan. But
she can never live up to his wife's memory…

Available wherever Harlequin books are sold.

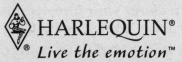

HARLEQUIN®
Live the emotion™

www.eHarlequin.com   HSRWM

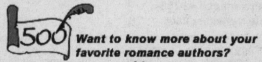

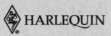
INTRIGUE®

COMING NEXT MONTH

#789 BULLETPROOF BILLIONAIRE by Mallory Kane
New Orleans Confidential
New Orleans Confidential agent Seth Lewis took on the alias of a suave international tycoon to infiltrate the Cajun Mob. He'd set out to gain entry by charming the rich widow Adrienne DeBlanc into telling him everything. It wasn't long before his protective instincts surfaced for the fragile beauty, but could he risk a high-stakes case for love?

#790 MIDNIGHT DISCLOSURES by Rita Herron
Nighthawk Island
In one tragic moment, radio psychologist Dr. Claire Kos had lost everything. She survived, only to become a serial killer's next target. Blind and vulnerable to attack, she turned to FBI agent Mark Steele—the man she'd loved and lost. As the killer took aim, Mark was poised to protect the woman he couldn't live without.

#791 ON THE LIST by Patricia Rosemoor
Club Undercover
Someone wanted to silence agent Renata Fox for good. She knew the Feds had accused the wrong person of being the Chicago sniper, but her speculations had somehow landed her on the real killer's hit list. So when Gabriel Connor showed up claiming he was on the assassin's trail, Renata knew she had to put her life—and her heart—in Gabe's hands....

#792 A DANGEROUS INHERITANCE by Leona Karr
Eclipse
When a storm delivered heiress Stacy Ashford into the iron-hard embrace of Josh Spencer, it seemed their meeting was fated. Gaining her inheritance depended on reopening the eerie hotel where Josh's kid sister died. And even though Stacy's inheritance bound them to an ever-tightening coil of danger, would Josh's oath to avenge his sister cost him the one woman who truly mattered?

#793 INTENSIVE CARE by Jessica Andersen
When Dr. Ripley Davis saw another of her patients flatline, she knew someone was killing the people in her care. But before she could find the real murderer, overbearing, impossibly sexy police officer Zachary Cage accused her of the crime. It wasn't long before her fiery resolve convinced him she wasn't the prime suspect...she was the prime *target*.

#794 SUDDEN ALLIANCE by Jackie Manning
When undercover operative Liam O'Shea found Sarah Regis on the side of the road, battered and incoherent, his razor-sharp instincts warned him she was in danger. As an amnesic murder witness, her only hope for survival was to stay in close proximity to Liam. Would their sudden alliance survive the secrets she'd kept locked inside?

www.eHarlequin.com

HICNM0704